Lessons in the Valley II:

Dissolution of the Marriage Mask

Dr. Tiffany C. Anderson

DIXON
PUBLISHING

The Publishing Midwife
DixonPublishingCompany.com

Colorado • Louisiana • DC
Texas • India • Africa

515-99-BOOKS

Copyright 2022 Dr. Tiffany Anderson
Title: Lessons in the Valley II: Dissolution of the Marriage Mask

Published by Dixon Publishing Company
Aurora, Colorado

Dixon Publishing Company, LLC,
P. O. Box 32023
Aurora, CO 80041
www.DixonPublishingCompany.com

Title:Lessons in the Valley II: Dissolution of the Marriage Mask
Cover Design: Robert Benson
Author's Photographer: Gary Davis
Interior Designer: Tracy Fagan
Editor: Sherrie Sutton
Audio Director: Linda C. Shaw
Press Kit: Beatrice Bruno
Press Kit Designer: Aishwary Tiwari

ISBN: 978-1-958735-06-0 (paperback)
ISBN: 978-1-958735-07-7 (hard back)

Table of Contents

Dedication

Dear God,

Thank you

I dedicate this book to those who have once again found themselves in a valley relearning the lessons that only the valley can teach, to those who have experienced the inevitable harm that results from being in a toxic or abusive relationship, to those whose reports have gone dismissed or ignored, to those who have questioned themselves and wondered whether the abuse was real, and to those who are or have been too ashamed to speak out. I will speak for you.

Finally, I dedicate this book to my daughter, Madison Grace Henley. I pray that you manifest true and genuine love all the days of your life keeping God first and 1 Corinthians 13:5 tucked away in your heart:

"Love is patient, Love is kind. It does not envy, it does not boast, it is not proud. It is not rude, it is not self-seeking, it is not easily angered, it keeps no record of wrongs. Love does not delight in evil but rejoices with the truth. It always protects, always trusts, always hopes, always perseveres. Love never fails"

1 Corinthians 13:5

A Message from the Author

"The Truth of the Matter"

The truth of the matter is anytime we are brave enough to publish a book instructing others on how to live through and overcome adversity, life will eventually present us with a personal opportunity to prove just how much we believe the advice we have given.

The truth of the matter is that the stories we fictionalize to protect the sanctity of an idealized hope may actually be based on a true story… our story.

The truth of the matter is that when you are in a position to motivate and encourage people using your life as a guide, you have a responsibility to show up with the truth, the whole truth, and nothing but the truth.

The truth of the matter is that when you are in a position to empower and heal others, you don't get to show up with the pretty parts of your story while keeping the ugly parts hidden. You see, the truth of the matter is that the ugliest, unedited parts of our story may very well be the parts that people need to see to help them overcome.

The truth of the matter is that while embellishment may sell books, the real unadulterated truth is what sets people free in God's time.

Wishing you love, peace, and light as you get set free. This is my truth.

-------Dr. Tiffany

This is a true story…my story. Names have been changed to protect the true identities of those involved. Actual names that are used are done so with permission. The information contained in this book does not take the place of professional counseling services.

TRIGGER WARNING: Some parts of my story may trigger emotional distress. My story is shared for the purposes of recognizing harmful relationship patterns and empowering you to overcome them. Please seek professional counseling services if you experience enduring psychological discomfort.

Introduction:
Once Upon a Time in Real Life

The long-awaited marriage between Faye and Love had finally happened. The hotel venue was well decorated. The limo was parked outside as the couple said their I do's in the presence of God, friends, and family. Faye was a beautiful bride filled with excitement as she witnessed her wedding day come to fruition. Love was a handsome groom who appeared happy to be marrying such a gorgeous bride. Captivated by Love's persistence in winning her over, they married on a beautiful sunny day in June. They spent five glorious days in Hawaii on their honeymoon. Finally, Faye had found a man who was patient, kind, and one that loved all of the heaviness of who she was. She was walking on sunshine!

Love was patient with her as she slowly made the decision to yoke herself with him. After so many failed relationships, Faye wanted to be sure to get it right this time. She found a sense of peace in Love's soft-spoken, almost shy demeanor. He was a sweet and gentle lover who bombed her with gifts and special attention both before and during the marriage. He even surprised his bride with a brand new, fully-loaded Range Rover for their first wedding anniversary. Even though Faye was not one who required things, she appreciated his gentle displays of kindness.

They were the ultimate power couple. Faye worked full time as a real estate agent while Love worked full time as an attorney and was working to open his own practice. Faye admired Love for being a good provider and protector. She also admired his ambition and the fact that he worked just as hard as she did. Although both contributed to the household bills and split everything straight down the middle, Love never pressured Faye about bills and money. He was the ultimate provider.

Although the couple took turns cooking, Faye was all too happy to have Love's plate waiting for him after his hard day at work. They spent time each day in conversation getting to know each other on a deeper level or just watching TV. Love protected and defended Faye and wasn't afraid to hurt someone else's feelings to protect hers. Faye felt safe to share all of the deep secrets of her past relationship failures, as well as her present fears, and insecurities with her husband. She trusted she had found the one who would love her forever, for better or for worse.

Unfortunately, this was short-lived. The marriage between Faye and Love would come to an end after just three short years. The ending of the marriage was set in motion by an argument over cleaning supplies. While cleaning supplies was clearly not the main issue, it was not unusual for such frivolous disagreements to initiate talk of divorce. Faye, now 30, would be forced to apply the lessons she had learned during her previous valley stays.

Like any marriage, there were disagreements and problems to be worked through. For some reason, the arguments between Faye and Love sparked over the smallest trivial matters such as laundry or Internet passwords and led to days or even weeks of no communication followed by talk of divorce. The root of the issues never really got addressed. They were left unresolved until a new disagreement occurred- and then brought up again only to be left unresolved then the cycle would continue.

With each passing disagreement, there began a sweet-mean cycle reflected in Love's behavior toward Faye. When things were good, they were really good. Love regularly showered Faye with love and affection which Faye loved and reciprocated. But in the blink of an argument's eye, he was able to shut off his love supply and quietly and deliberately withdraw his attention and affection from Faye. Love would go for weeks in cold indifference, pretending as though Faye was invisible. During these times, he spent more time away from home leaving his wife, Faye, alone. The covert, hollow responses Faye received from attempts to re-establish harmony in the marriage secretly crushed her spirit and self-esteem. Faye, while imperfect, considered herself a good person, a forgiving person. However, the circular conversation, finger-pointing, and character attacks during arguments with Love drove Faye to question her own good nature. With each passing phase of deliberate disconnection, it became more difficult for her to figure out which side of Love to believe– the Love that was sweet to her during good times or the Love that could so easily withdraw, retreat, and emotionally abandon her during a crisis. Faye went from walking on sunshine to walking on eggshells.

Arguments between Faye and Love became more frequent. Small disagreements led to days of severed communication. Faye and Love would stand together at their double vanity bathroom mirror or walk through their 5000 square foot mansion preparing for the day with neither of them saying a word. The silent treatment tended to come easy for Love. He was able to go for long stretches of time this way. Faye tried to play this game but would eventually fail and break the ice after only a few days. Faye recognized this type of behavior as toxic, even painful. She couldn't understand how any healthy-minded person could live this way.

Faye would break the ice by initiating small talk or even attempting to have a civilized conversation about the unsettled issue. This often resulted in finger-pointing and new arguments about past grievances that Love stored in his arsenal of violations he kept tucked in the back of his mind.

In a desperate attempt to reconnect, Faye once tried to initiate prayer. Coaching him to connect in prayer, Faye grabbed hold of Love's limp hand. Peering out of one partially closed eye, she noticed that he wouldn't even so much as bow his head or close his eyes as she prayed.

As each phase of the silent treatment passed, Love found it easier to ignore Faye, to not even speak to her when he walked in the house. If he was upset, he refused to eat any meals she prepared, purposely leaving his untouched plate on the counter. Stonewalling, Faye learned, was his weapon of choice. The cracks in his soft-spoken mask were starting to show.

Each conflict, no matter how small, brought with it even longer periods of disconnection. In addition to the silent treatment, a darker side of Love began to show—a nasty side that used Faye's past as ammunition during disagreements. After months of cold disregard, Faye took their daughter and left home for a week in an attempt to get out of the cold environment that was sending her into a valley of depression. Love didn't seem to notice or even care that they were gone. While it psychologically traumatized Faye, periods of disconnection and withdrawal came easy for Love, almost like he had done this before.

Faye was used to talking out problems and coming up with a strategic plan to resolve issues. This seemed difficult for Love as his entire narrative of who Faye was as a person would frequently change based on how he felt about Faye at the time. While Faye had her faults, all the good that she was and tried to be was quickly stomped out by any current violation and sandwiched between transgressions from the past. The sentencing and re-sentencing phase began as Faye unknowingly racked up a laundry list of charges stored in Love's violation vault for the next argument. Faye felt hopeless, powerless, depressed, and emotionally abandoned. She was drained. She was falling apart.

Following the cleaning supply argument, Faye spent several nights sleeping in their guest room. This was her initial reaction to Love locking her out of the bedroom they shared. She later decided to use the incident as an opportunity to write, cry, engage in introspection, and heal.

Ten days later, Faye reappeared from the guest room recharged and expecting to eventually have a dialogue as she returned to the marital bedroom. She was unaware; however, that Love had spent his ten days away from her dusting off and meditating on old grievances he had stored up in the violation vault over the entire course of their marriage. The cleaning supply incident was the perfect opportunity to unload his grievances and make the decision that he was done with the marriage. While Faye healed and searched for reasons to stay in the marriage, Love searched through the violation vault to identify reasons to walk away.

As she sat alone writing, Love entered the room without so much as a look in Faye's direction. More silence. Faye once again tried to play his game. It was crippling to her. She was slowly suffocating from lack of connection. No matter how she tried, she could not seem to bring herself to live this way.

Aware of his evasive energy, Faye noticed that Love no longer wore his wedding band. Love removing his wedding ring had been a clear indication in times past that the marriage was over; he was done with her. Faye went into a familiar panic: fear of being abandoned and fear that this time was the end.

In response to his threats to leave, she cried, pleaded, or tried to convince him to stay and work through the problems together in lieu of throwing the entire marriage away.

"For better or for worse...remember? She would say. Not this time. Faye was tired and had had enough of the childish behaviors of the marriage.

This time she calmly inquired, "I see that you are not wearing your wedding ring again. Is this the direction that we are going now?"

"Yup," he said casually. His cavalier, nonchalant tone wounded and angered Faye at the same time. His cold indifference following disagreements was becoming all too common. He didn't even look in her direction as he chewed a piece of toast and walked out the door. Faye felt hurt at the thought that she hadn't even been worth a conversation, but angrier about his casual response.

Like so many of Love's decisions, Faye was just supposed to know what was going on in his mind. There had been no known infidelity or major financial hardship; no real grounds for divorce Faye could think of. If being unhappy was grounds for divorce, then Faye had plenty of grounds.

Deep down inside, Faye wanted her marriage. She felt they could work through these things and held onto hope that the storm would pass. She wanted a loving marriage like the ones she had witnessed with the marriages of her friends and the connection and care they appeared to have for one another. Instead, a dark cloud of silence hung over her marriage resulting in periods of anxiety, depression, and even Post Traumatic Stress symptoms for her.

Love had now become cold. His nonchalant energy felt like one wounding blowback to the valley floor. Faye's self-esteem secretly crumbled. She found herself grateful for mediocre treatment such as Love leaving out an extra bath towel for her or telling her where he was going when he left the house like he normally would. In periods of discord, all of this stopped. It wounded Faye even deeper when Love didn't even bring himself to honor her on her birthday. This was so different from the man who showered her with small gifts for no reason during the beginning of their relationship. Now, Faye was not even worth a birthday card.

Fears of the little girl living inside of Faye resurfaced…the little girl who Faye thought she had found, re-parented, and taken such good care of. The little girl's cries were back; sadly, this time her cries were heard and felt deep within the marrow of Faye's bones.

I'm being thrown away, she thought. He doesn't care.

Faye found herself resisting the urge to beg Love for a connection, to beg Love for a conversation, or the urge to give Love her body so she wouldn't be discarded or left alone. Faye recognized that her impulse to respond this way was an attempt to survive and relieve the anxiety which came as a result of Love's detachment and withdrawal. It was like he no longer valued her, and it hurt.

Faye now found herself meditating on all the unsettled, frivolous disagreements that had become all too common throughout the course of the marriage. The intrusive mental memories looped and re-looped in her head as she unsuccessfully tried to shut them out. A silent movie played in her mind of the time Love kicked her to the floor during an escalated argument. He put her in a bear hug in an attempt to keep her from leaving. In an effort to get free of his hold, she accidentally hit him in the nose. It really was an accident, but Love did not see it that way.

In response, Love gave himself permission to lift his leg and kick Faye to the floor as she unsuspectedly walked away, her belongings in tow. She had no idea that Love's size 12 foot was coming right at her lower back. Her fall to the floor mentally played in slow motion, recalling how the contents of her purse fell to the floor with her in a loud thump. As she rose to fight back, she was flooded with mental commercials containing questions about why she would stay in a marriage where this type of fighting was necessary.

The episode when Love brandished a taser from his pocket during a heated argument flashed across her mental movie screen. While Love never actually pointed the taser directly at her, there was a deliberate display and visibility of a weapon in an attempt to intimidate her. This was enough to create the desired effect: FEAR.

The scene when Love locked Faye out of their home clashed with the scene where he left her stranded at a local hospital emergency room at 2 a.m. as she waited for a good friend to make their transition. The memory of the time she lay crying on the bathroom floor flashed in her mind as memories of Love walking in to change clothes without so much as a look in her direction let alone acknowledgement of her pain. Finally, the periods of his deliberate disconnection and coldness rolled like ending movie credits to her traumatic memories.

Faye was left with the lingering thought, "Was this my fault?"

Faye was no wuss. Her previously toxic relationships had taught her to protect herself, even to lash out when threatened. This sometimes meant saying not-so-nice and even ugly things to Love in response to his flaming arrows. When talking calmly didn't seem effective, Faye used words like petty and childish to describe Love's behavior. Love twisted these words. Suddenly Faye was the abuser. She once got so angry with this behavior, she told him he was acting like a punk and needed to grow up. As she always did, Faye took responsibility for her words and quickly apologized. To no avail, Love stored these events in his mental violation vault where he could easily reproduce them as exhibits A, B, and C during the sentencing phase.

They tried therapy, first with the church, then with a professional. Faye initiated both. Instead of seeing Faye's genuine attempt to revive their marriage in cardiac arrest, she was accused of trying to make Love look bad. Each argument, Faye quickly forgave. When she was wrong, as she sometimes was, Faye was quick to apologize and open to talking it out. She just wanted peace. But Love was unforgiving. He kept score of wrongs and would rather prove a point than work together with Faye..

While Faye tried to position herself toward reconciliation, Love seemed to position himself on opposite sides using past violations to justify current behavior. With each argument came a laundry list of mistakes Faye had made throughout the course of the three-year marriage, presented as exhibit A no matter how frivolous. Love was harsh in his sentencing, using her past as ammunition, leaving Faye with the resounding message that she wasn't and would never be good enough.

"That's why he didn't want you. If it was not for me, you wouldn't even be married." Love's Words resounded in Faye's head on the big speaker of her mind as she subconsciously absorbed all the negative messages about herself that Love intended to leave.

Not good enough. Discarded. Replaceable. No value. Unlovable.

If she was honest with herself, she would admit that many of those thoughts were pre-existing. The original cuts from her previous wounds left a stain on her heart. Love's behavior, while hurtful, was only highlighting what was already there. He would once again disconnect, going on about his day-to-day life, leaving Faye feeling broken, bruised, and this time, discarded. She could not help but wonder how Love could be so kind and loving one minute and so cold and indifferent the next. Faye wondered if he ever really loved her.

Faye stayed in the marriage silently hoping Love would see that despite their problems, she was still good and worth keeping. She wanted to be loved and certainly didn't want the embarrassment of a divorce mark on her relationship report card.

Love took no accountability for any of the problems in the marriage. In his mind, his character allowed him to do no wrong. Any potential wrongs were either justified or minimized. In the end, everything was Faye's fault, right down to the termination of the marriage. Each argument became a word salad of Faye's faults and an ongoing circular conversation she struggled to keep track of. He had this way of spinning her words into pictures of deliberate deception and lies. She tried to defend herself by reminding him of his faults. His responses felt like wounding blows.

"Man, get the fuck out of here with that! This is all on you! I will handle the divorce this week." This was one of many instances in which Love threatened Faye with divorce. This always seemed to be the only option on the table each time leaving Faye feeling disposable, unlovable, and not good enough.

She was always puzzled by how easily Love could curse at her and speak to her like a man on the street during his emotional tantrums. "Man, get the fuck outta here," sounded again in Faye's mind. Those were his final words to her before he stormed away with the plan of filing for divorce. Faye silently cried inside as she heard his motorcycle start and he backed out of the driveway. The tears were slow to reach her eyes. Her chest burned with the pain of abandonment that she remembered all too well.

"Mama, are you ok? I can smell your tears," their young daughter Lillian often said to her during moments of her attempts to mask her emotional pain.

Contrary to what Faye saw her mother do, her daughter, Lillian, often saw her cry. Sometimes Faye tried to hold back her emotions; many times, she simply could not. This was one of those times.

Lillian watched as the tears finally spilled over. Faye wanted to call her own mother. She wanted to reach out to her for support. But it felt better to be where she was than to be met with emotional unavailability and a stern expectation for her to simply stand up, be strong, and be thankful for her blessings. Faye needed to bury her face in her mother's chest and cry. She needed to be broken. The little girl inside of Faye needed her mommy.

17

After regaining control of her emotions, Faye began to read, pray, and reflect on the lessons in the valley she had previously learned. Her sudden fall to the valley floor had shaken her so that she had almost forgotten them. She realized that while Love demonstrated his ability to live under the same roof in cold silence, she could not go on this way. She certainly did not want to reflect this way of being for her daughter. The cold silence slowly chipped away at her self-worth and self-esteem, resulting in post-traumatic stress symptoms. She had lost any semblance of joy and peace. Faye mustered up enough strength to remind herself that her destiny was not tied to anyone who left her, not even Love.

Her prayers for God's direction yielded a familiar scripture: But if the unbeliever leaves, let it be so. The brother or sister is not bound in such circumstances; God has called us to live in peace (1 Corinthians 7:15). It was time to let go.

While she loved her husband, Faye was no longer willing to remain in a marriage where passive violence and divorce were such immediate solutions to marital problems. She was no longer willing to remain in a marriage where she was constantly sentenced and re-sentenced for past offenses. She wanted a marriage with a man who was willing to work through problems together. She wanted a marriage where both people were accountable for their contribution to issues, each apologizing when they were wrong.

Faye was no longer willing to beg, plead, and cry for genuine communication and conflict resolution. She wanted a marriage of forgiveness and genuine acceptance of apologies. She wanted a partner strong enough to love her through conflict and stay in the fight for the marriage as opposed to staying to fight each other. She wanted her for better or for worse,but told herself the truth: This would not come to pass in the emotionally and psychologically abusive relationship she was currently in.

Faye gave up on her dream of hearing Love say, "Baby, let's talk." She accepted that stonewalling was the only card Love knew how to play. For the first time in her marriage, she imagined her life separate and apart from Love; it didn't hurt so bad.

What Faye soon realized was that Love had never emotionally grown up or attached himself to her in the way she had emotionally attached to him. This was why it was so easy for him to detach–It wasn't real. It never was. Faye realized that what she truly desired would never come from the abusive relationship she found herself in.

Love was always so sweet in the eyes of her friends and family; shy even. Who would believe the covert narcissistic abuse she never saw coming? Who would ever believe her when she finally revealed to friends and family that she had been in an abusive marriage?

Faye couldn't worry about that now. The damage had been done. She was done! So, with the courage and strength God gave her, she freed Love to leave. While it pained her, there came with it a sense of relief. This time Faye chose herself and walked away with her dignity and the goal of becoming who God called her to be. She realized she should have left sooner and forgave herself for not doing so. She also forgave Love for not being who she needed him to be.

The story ended with Faye reentering the valley–the Valley of Divorce. This would be a new valley with new lessons to be learned about herself, love's true identity, and where love actually lived. She would know exactly what love looked like next time it came around.

"The truth is that love is supportive and nurturing, not aggressive or demanding. It is protective, not overwhelming. Love expands, gives, and heals."
----Iyanla Vanzant

Chapter 1
Flashbacks from the Passenger Seat

There I was, still married and holding on to Love. The divorce never happened although Love's threats of it never stopped. At every argument, Love used the threat of divorce which tampered at my old abandonment wounds. I sat in the passenger seat of his Ford F150. Something about my seating arrangement that day gave me deja vu. I had recently acknowledged Love for helping me to discover the motivation I needed to break free of fear, discover my power, and to be pushed into my destiny of overcoming my own emotional scars. What was hidden from view was the fact that the motivation I gave him credit for was conceived and birthed from a secret; a secret that was originally intended to protect my union by casting Love in a role that hid his true identity in my story. Yet, there I was, doing something that I had encouraged the world and promised myself that I would never do again… beg for love, beg a man to stay to fight for us. To see that despite my flaws, I still had value. I thought I had completed this valley and finished my lesson. I soon realized that just because a lesson is finished doesn't necessarily mean that the lesson is complete.

The salt for my tears swelled my face and dried my mouth. I clenched my chest and listened again to the piercing words that brought back familiar bodily sensations I had felt before in valleys in the past. This time they were stronger. The little girl inside cried again at the sound of Love's words.

"I'm not happy. I don't want to be married anymore" said Love, my husband of the last five years.

This was not the first time he had spoken these words to me. It seemed like every disagreement led us down this path and I was being confronted and threatened with the possibility of divorce. Every argument, no matter how trivial, was fatal and led to a combination of ways Love would communicate the same wounding message. He didn't want me or our marriage anymore. Love seemed to always be pulling for a way out of our marriage. Meanwhile, I constantly found myself in a position of tug of war pulling for reasons to reconcile and stay together despite my deteriorating emotional health. It seemed like I was always exchanging my emotional well-being for my desire to be loyal to an unfruitful marriage. This time was no different. Although I had heard threats of divorce from Love multiple times throughout our brief marriage, this time was more painful. Maybe it was the fact that his final announcement of divorce came on the very day of our fifth-year wedding anniversary. His desire would echo again three days later as we sat in his truck with me hoping to talk things over; him with a made-up mind that he wanted to leave. I tightly held onto the passenger's door handle preparing for the next round of verbal blows from his repeated words.

"I'm tired. I'm not happy. I just don't want to be married anymore," Love repeated himself, not even looking in my direction.

Three days earlier he was telling me how much he loved me and wanted our marriage to work. I was telling him the same thing as we cuddled in a heated pool in Cancun, Mexico in celebration of our fifth-year wedding anniversary. Days later, all of that changed. As I sat in the passenger seat of his truck I wrestled in my mind with how things between us could always go from hot to cold so fast and so drastically. I wrestled with which version of Love to believe…the shy, caring and gentle version whom I first met, or the cold, cruel, unattached person I had come to know and was seeing on this day as I sat in the passenger seat.

I wept uncontrollably as I tried again to digest the bitter information falling from his lips. Remnants of TD Jakes' sermon I once referred to called, *"LET THEM GO,"* flashed in my mind. An internal voice whispered, *"Your destiny is not tied to the person who left, remember?"* My mental grip on that message was lost as I continued to weep. A sudden desperation to reach for Love's hand came over me hoping it would help him recall his love for me or *any* love that was left. When I reached for his hand it was limp, cold and disconnected. It reminded me of the time I tried to reconcile with him through prayer after one of our many petty arguments. He would not so much as bow his head or close his eyes as I prayed for us that day.

Love remained silent and looked straight ahead; disconnected, stoic and void of any empathy or emotion. My breathing became labored as the tears continued to fall while my detached husband remained silent. He later reached into his center console and retrieved a brown, wrinkled paper towel. He placed it on my thigh, I assume for me to wipe my swelling face, and returned his attention forward like that of a military soldier assuming the position. He remained emotionally detached, maintaining a cold, robotic-like nature.

"I'm not happy" he continued, looking straight ahead. "You deserve to be with someone who will be happy with you. I don't want this marriage anymore." His words took another wounding blow leaving a deep ache in my chest. This time his words fused with a report of every single thing I had ever done "wrong" in the marriage. Everything I had done and not done was pulled from the fault vault that Love kept in the back of his mind and laid out for examination. Exhibit A, B, C.... I was back on trial.

"I'm not happy. I'm telling you I'm not happy. I haven't had any peace for five years."

His words gut punched me again, crushing my spirit. *The entire five years?* I thought to myself. I had been clueless of that. I too had definitely experienced periods of interrupted peace during the marriage, but to say that I had no peace or joy for the entire five years would have been a complete and total exaggeration of the truth...something Love was good at doing.

My mind began to shift in and out of the present moment as I went into mental flashbacks of events that occurred throughout the marriage. I thought about all the times I had been unhappy, lost *my* peace, and even considered leaving him. There had been multiple periods of unhappiness for me as well, leading to trauma, depression, and anxiety. A combination of fear and hope that God would save my marriage kept me there along with the belief that God wanted me to stay married to this man. I also carried a hope that one day I would be reunited with the person I met in the beginning. It never dawned on me to leave him based on feelings alone.

"We have both been unhappy at points in this marriage. That is no reason to quit," I pleaded with tears still falling from my face. "We are five years in; don't quit now."

"I'm not happy," Love repeated coldly.

I mentally recounted how unhappy and depressed I became following the time Love kicked me to the floor and down a flight of stairs during an argument. We were on what was supposed to be a blended family vacation in Orlando with my daughter and his youngest daughter. We had just returned from the theme park when yet another small disagreement resulted in his threats of divorce.

"You know what" he prefaced his developing threat, "You just need to find somebody else to be with. I want a divorce,"

I was too emotionally exhausted to respond or participate in this exchange. Additionally, I knew that to engage him at that point would only open the door to another round of rabbit hole arguing likely over some old grievance he had stored away in the fault vault of his mind until the perfect time. Frustrated and hurt with once again being threatened with divorce, I chose to disengage and made the decision to sleep in another room that night. I calmly informed Love of my decision as I tearfully collected my purse and other belongings to leave. It was then that I experienced my first episode of physical abuse in the marriage. I could feel my body tensing up as I mentally recalled the events of that night.

Love must have been reading my mind because this very incident was the next charge brought up on my docket. I had already been wrongfully convicted but now was being re-sentenced.

"You can't even take accountability for anything you do in this marriage," Love yelled. "Let me ask you a question. Say YES or NO. If you had not sucker punched me in my face that time, would I have picked my foot up and kicked you down? YES or NO? You made me do that! How can I stay with you if you can't even be honest and own that?"

Confusion and anger set in. I was also hurt that Love had found a way to justify picking up his foot and kicking me, his wife, while my back was turned to him. He was good at blame shifting and bringing up old grievances to support whatever position he stood in at the moment. Unfortunately, who I was as a person, a wife, a mother and my entire character was tightly wound up into those moments. Those circular conversations left me confused and tired. The little girl inside of me just wanted to be held and told that despite that incident, we would be ok. The adult part of me wanted to defend myself because I knew that his version of that event was simply not true. Yet, another part of me knew better than to go down that road with him; there would be no use. Conversations with Love were never about accountability, compromise, forgiveness, and solutions. They were always about competition, being right, and hinged on who would win.

After some consideration, I allowed the adult part of me to speak up. Up until that point, I was an emotional mess repeatedly asking him what *he* needed to be happy again and trying to convince him to fight for our marriage. Once again, I found myself exchanging my needs and mental well-being for a commitment I had made to the marriage. I desperately tried to understand *his* position while he continued to disregard mine. My hand pressed against the passenger seat where I sat. I spoke my truth.

"That is *not* what happened, and you know it" I said peacefully but firmly through my now drying tears. "You know full well that I was trying to leave the room. You bear hugged me and physically restrained me onto the bed to prevent me from leaving. Yes, I had to physically fight to get out of your grasp and *if* you were *accidently* hit in the process, I am sorry. But I never made a decision to intentionally hit you. I was trying to get free. I was walking away from you when you made a conscious decision to pick up your foot and kick me down. MY BACK WAS TURNED!" I yelled through new tears, my voice escalating a little as the unresolved trauma of that summer night in May set into my body.

The flash back continued. My mind flashed backward as I remembered visions of pink OPI nail polish, among other items, falling out of my purse with me as my body crashed to the floor in a loud thump. The impact of Love's kick to my lower back sent me crashing to the floor and half way down a flight of stairs. The roughness of the carpet scraped my hands and knees as I tried to brace my fall. I recalled how I got up seemingly in slow motion but fighting like a wild woman. I saw nothing but the top of Love's bald, freshly shaven head through a tinge of red as I swung and hemmed him up in the window blinds of our vacation bedroom. I was running on pure adrenaline and fighting for my life. I couldn't believe that my husband had done this. It wasn't until that adrenaline faded that I felt the sharp debilitating pains in my back and side which added a trip to the emergency room to our blended family vacation plans.

That night, Love's attitude shifted into care mode as he helped me down the stairs and into his truck. He expressed remorse as he drove me to a local Orlando hospital.

"I aint no good," he cried out, hitting the steering wheel with his fist as he drove. "If you want to leave me, I understand," he continued as he sped through red lights to get me to the emergency room. I watched as tears welled up in his eyes like two puddles. It was the first and only time I could remember him crying. Oddly, there was a part of me that wanted to console *him*. He had kicked me and there I was having an emotional tug of war with my little girl self who wanted to hug and makeup and my adult self who knew that this was not ok. The thumping pain from my back and side snapped me back into reality and prevented me from acting on my urge to console him.

I was filled with both emotional and physical pain. I still could not believe this had happened. For a brief moment, I considered calling the police. My uncertainty about the domestic violence law in Florida and worries about what would happen to the girls who were still at the hotel clouded my judgment. I prayed that it was all a dream. I screamed. I cried all the way to the emergency room that night. I wept at the top of my lungs as I tried to digest the reality of that night and considered what I would tell the emergency room staff once we got to the hospital. I didn't want to tell on Love, even though his actions had landed me there.

"I fell down the stairs," I lied to the hospital staff. That was one of the lowest points in my life.

I thought about the girls back at the vacation condo who were probably scared to death. How would I explain this? What questions would they have? What was I going to tell Madison about why I had eventually decided to stay with a man who had kicked me down like a dog in anger?

I slept on the sofa bed in the living room area of our vacation condo that night. Love slept in the master bedroom while the girls stayed in the room they shared. As I lay there crying, I considered leaving him but the truth was I wanted to forgive him. I didn't want to believe that he was this person. I just wanted him to apologize and assure me that it would never happen again so that we could move on.

While there was no apology, he did try to be comforting and accommodating the next day. The kind, gentle, caring Love was back, trying to apply heated towels to my injuries and seemingly interested in my well-being. He acted as though nothing had ever happened. I almost got swooped away by his kind gestures forgetting that not 24 hours ago he was threatening me with divorce and kicking me to the floor. The same person who had wounded me was now trying to heal me. Part of me wanted it for some dysfunctional reason I would come to understand later. But Love's kindness was short-lived as he gradually morphed back into the cruel man I had come to know and recognize. It started when I declined to attend a scheduled time share where he would forfeit a 100.00 deposit. Things quickly escalated when I initiated discussion of the elephant in the room. When I held him accountable for his behavior and referred to his blind kick as cowardly Love quickly turned back into the monster I had seen the night

27

before. He conveniently found a way to make me responsible for my own abuse that day.

"You made me kick you!" he yelled that day as he took off his wedding ring and told me he wanted a divorce. Unsurprisingly, he gave me the silent treatment for the remainder of the vacation. Even in my trauma and unhappiness of that night, I made a decision to forgive Love and never brought that incident up again. In doing that, I also failed to set any boundaries.

My flashback came to an end and my mind shifted back to the present moment remembering my passenger seat position.

"Even then I forgave you and never brought it up again because I love you," I whispered softly as I slowly calmed down and finished my account of that night. I was hoping this would be a good segue for agreement and reconnection. I was wrong. In his normal way, he defended and justified his bad behavior taking no accountability for his actions.

"I didn't bear hug you!" He defended himself. "I pinned you down on the bed to keep you from leaving. But you could have gotten up without hitting me! That was all your fault! Take accountability!"

His ongoing accusations, shaming, and blame faded into incoherent muffles as his eyes bucked and darkened. Saliva flew from his mouth as he verbally laid out my charges. He was like a demon; a demon I would later learn was real.

As my mind shifted again, I wondered whatever happened to the shy, kind, sweet guy who had met me at Target with a slice of his mother's pound cake because I didn't want him to know where I lived while he was trying to court me or the man who would send me love songs through social media to randomly to express his love for me via text. Was any of it even real? The gentle, quiet guy who my family and friends knew was shedding his skin again as the blame and accusations continued.

"You come home from work every day and I am afraid to ask you how your day was because I know it's going to be negative energy," Love continued my list of charges.

Love didn't work. He had quit his day job shortly after we were married and had convinced a therapist somewhere that he was unable to work due to injuries he suffered while in the National Guard. This provided him the luxury of staying home every day to collect a check. I wasn't so lucky. I worked two jobs which consisted of 10-hour work days. Even then, I had to pay him half of everything. I didn't want to work like that and I certainly had not expected to live like roommates with my husband. But he made it clear that I was responsible for taking care of myself. So, I worked to do just that. I can admit that there were indeed days when I came home exhausted, sad, and even irritable for having to work so hard. Adding to my irritability was the fact that Love saw how hard I worked, yet he stayed home each day drinking coffee and playing candy crush.

I never came home raising hell. If anything, I would come home more withdrawn, depressed and not up for much conversation. I was tired. I would engage in the normal pleasantries, take a shower, do my best to help Madison with her homework, eat or not eat, and then go to bed. Up until that point I had been unaware of his negative interpretation of my routine, let alone my entire character during those times. I didn't consider that I was behaving badly. *"Was I that bad? Did this warrant divorce?"* I mentally asked myself.

Love had further re-wrote history and convinced himself that during my after-work interactions with Madison, he had heard laughter and fun, but with him I would come home and offer negative energy. I knew that was untrue; however, when you are in a relationship with a toxic person, you will find that you become too exhausted to defend yourself against the constant twisting of their facts which would play itself out again and again.

Present, past, present, past....my mind continued to vacillate as Love continued to lay out my list of charges which, to him, had all contributed to the failure of our marriage. According to him, none of it was his fault.

The flashbacks resumed. This time, they played like movies in color. I remembered the hand gun being removed from Love's aqua blue-colored pair of shorts during an argument. He had pulled the gun out of his pocket and held it by his side. He stared me in my face, almost daring me without words to try him.

"I will blow your MF brains out," I recalled him saying. His words rang in my ear.

"But I did not point it at you," I remember him defending his behavior. That too was minimized and justified. Again, I failed to set boundaries.

Another flash! I recalled the hospital walls as I sat stranded at a local ER at 2 am. Love had gotten upset and left me there. Madison's father was dying of cancer and I had been called to be there to discuss plans for Madison. Love initially offered to drive me. But once again, some unknown perceived slight on my part justified him abandoning me at the hospital in the middle of the night.

"Go back in there with yo man and his family," he mocked as I followed him to his truck to retrieve my purse. I then watched as he drove off and I made my way back into the hospital. An acquaintance of mine, Cynthia, came later and gave me a ride home that night. When I returned home around 3:30 a.m. Love was sleeping peacefully in bed.

This was not the first time he had abandoned me. My mind flashed to the time I asked Love to take me to the emergency room. I was experiencing severe side pain that night. I hesitated to ask. We had had a recent argument a few days prior resulting in his typical response of cold disconnection and him staying away from home. I knew it was easy for him to withdraw love and affection when we had a disagreement. However, I thought for sure that during a potential medical emergency, this would be different. Love's response to my request crushed my spirit.

"Call the ambulance, I am in Vicksburg at the casino," he replied before hanging up the phone in my face.

I ended up driving myself to the emergency room that night. Once again, when I returned home after I was discharged, I found Love resting in bed watching Sports Center.

My mind shifted again. There I was standing outside of Madison's bedroom window knocking in the middle of the night. Love had locked me out of the marital home after I refused to engage him during an exchange that was escalating. I decided instead to disengage and take a walk to the corner to clear my mind. I didn't think I needed to take my keys. I returned 10 minutes later to find the garage closed and all the doors locked.

"Mama, did he lock you out?" Madison asked as she opened the front door to let me in.

"No," I lied again. "I locked myself out."

Yet there I remained sitting in the passenger seat of his truck pleading with him to fight for our marriage. But why? Love kept bringing up my charges while I kept forgiving him of his. I wondered how I got back to this valley. I considered the strong possibility that I had never left.

"You didn't… your fault, take responsibility, I'm not happy" Love's words again disappeared into muffles as though I were slowly sinking underwater. My thoughts shifted back to how quickly we had gotten together and gotten married. I wanted my happily ever after so badly that I had failed to get to know this side of him and convinced myself that he was the one God kept for me. Dread set in as I realized my error.

I couldn't speak. I felt paralyzed in a fog that day in the passenger seat. I vacillated between fear, obligation, and guilt. *Was I that bad?* I wanted to defend myself against Love's twisted accusations but I knew to do so would only open another rabbit's hole of crazy-making conversation. It would also defeat my intentions of reconciliation which was my ultimate goal in the truck that day. As my mind shifted and unshifted, I thought about a quote I once read that said, "If you don't let go of someone when it's time, God will allow them to continue to hurt you until you do." Maybe this was the case for me…I was certainly in a lot of pain. But we can fix this, I thought.

This, I thought to myself. What was *this* even about this time? What could have possibly happened to lead to divorce this time? How was it always so easy for him to abandon ship and leave? I asked myself these questions as he continued to lay out all of my imperfections. His angry words again disappeared into under-water muffles and my mind shifted away.

"How did I get back here?" I thought. I was filled with shame as I reflected on how just a few months earlier, I had written and released a book on overcoming the cycle of relationship woundedness. Yet, there I was with my wounds reopened, gaping, exposed, and stinking right there in the passenger seat where I sat. My mother's words began to ring in my ear as my mind shifted again.

"Tiffany, only you know when enough is enough."

Was she right? Wasn't I supposed to be a forgiving Christian wife? I was always willing to stay in the ring with Love. But while I was looking for a reason to stay, Love was looking for a way out.

All the pain of what I had experienced throughout the five-year marriage came flooding back at once. I resisted. I didn't want to accept responsibility for who I had chosen to marry and what I had allowed to continue. I didn't want to admit to people that I had been in an emotionally and sometimes physically abusive marriage. I didn't want to admit that in my first book, I deliberately left out what was happening in my marriage using fictionalized characters Faye and Love. I held on to hope of getting back the man I had first met. I wanted things to go back to the way they used to be. Deep down I knew it could never go back. It was over. It was then that I realized that sometimes in order to understand the present, you have to take a look at the past.

Chapter 2
Happy Anniversary! I want a Divorce

March 19. It was a light rainy day in Cancun, Mexico. The previous days in Cancun had been sunny and warm; this day we were not so lucky. Love and I made the best of our fifth-year wedding anniversary by sitting on the balcony of our Cancun hotel room overlooking the water. Up until this point, Love and I had had a rocky marriage. I had heard from other married couples that after the fifth-year marital hiccups, things got easier. I held on hoping that would be my truth. I was willing to grow and hoped that he would be willing also. I even had this vision of God healing our marriage and us writing a book together to help other couples heal their broken marriages.

"Soooooo, are you going to post anything special today?" I teasingly inquired of him referring to his annual anniversary post of a love song to acknowledge our anniversary. His love affirmations were one of the things that made me fall in love with him. It made me feel like he really cared.

"Are *you* going to post anything? Did *you* post anything today? Love replied to me callously. It wasn't nice. It was antagonizing and mean in tone. It hurt! A familiar ache ran across my chest again. I recalled the days that he would acknowledge us without me asking. That always gave me hope that we would be ok. He was always posting about other people's birthdays and celebrating their special occasions. I thought for sure that the day of our wedding anniversary would be special enough.

Maybe there was a selfish part of me that wanted to be recognized by my husband on our anniversary. I wanted to feel special to him again like I was in the beginning. This would also be a small confirmation that he still loved me. But today was not that day. My feelings were hurt by his response.

I excused myself and had a private cry in the restroom of our hotel before returning to the balcony. I returned to our balcony seats wearing shades. I was hoping to conceal the fact that I had been crying. My emotions seemed to always upset Love. I didn't want him to get upset or think I was trying to start problems as I had been accused of doing in times past. My red nose must have given me away because his energy became even more avoidant. He looked uncomfortable and excused himself inside.

"My socks are getting wet. I'm going inside," he said as he stood to leave.

I recognized his evasive energy. I paused for a moment noticing that there was no rain on our balcony to wet his socks.

"Come on, let's go in and watch a movie," he said as he interrupted my pause.

Me and my red nose accompanied Love back inside our hotel room. In efforts to conceal my tears, I kept my shades on my face. Although to anyone else this may have seemed odd, he never said a word. I wanted to talk, to reconnect, to lay on his chest and talk about the direction of our marriage. I needed reassurance. The last five years had been tough and I was hoping for a rebirth. But there we were on our fifth-year wedding anniversary sitting in the bed watching TV with me holding back tears behind shades.

I realize that I could have initiated that conversation, but I was afraid. I was afraid that if I expressed how I truly felt it was going to turn into an argument or I would be accused of creating a problem. That was certainly not my intent. I wanted him to understand that my tears were not about a social media post as he later so conveniently twisted. I wanted him to understand that those tears were tears of disappointment that we had not progressed further than we were and the thought that I did not have my loving husband anymore.

I reflected on the times when Love would celebrate me and us on my birthdays or other special occasions. He would post a love song and tag me in it or send it to my phone. I felt so special and loved by small things like that. He would give me a handwritten card and I would read the words over and over again. I didn't require much in the way of things. Small gestures were often enough to make me feel like I was his "special lady." But now, five years into the marriage, it felt like I was no longer worthy of that. Those loving social media birthday posts he once shared had now turned into posts that read "Happy Birthday to my headache." After five years of marriage, it felt like we were growing farther apart instead of closer together. This was a painful awareness that brought me to tears that day of our fifth year wedding anniversary in Mexico. Tears, which unfortunately, Love viewed as a form of manipulation rather than a genuine expression of the emotional pain that I was in.

I rehearsed in my mind ways to present the conversation without any tears but decided against each delivery. As I attempted to maintain control of my emotions the tears continued to fall. I excused myself back to the balcony. I just didn't feel safe crying in his presence. I had learned to keep my tears and emotions inside or hidden in order to avoid conflict. I sat on the balcony chair of our hotel that day and grieved the loss of the marriage I had hoped would be.

"What's wrong with you?" He mirrored empathy as he walked onto the balcony about ten minutes later. His sudden arrival startled me and something about his concern felt less than genuine. It felt mocking and almost rehearsed. But I was willing to accept it. It was better than nothing.

I remember being afraid to answer him… to give him the honest response of what I was feeling. I knew it would not be well received and would somehow turn into an argument. I didn't want that. I just wanted the person I met in the beginning back again. Against my better judgment, I tearfully spoke my truth and shared the feelings that had accumulated in my heart and mind about his lack of effort and concern that day.

"You are a fucking narcissist! All this over social media! I want a divorce!" Love's words rang in my ears. He had convinced himself that my tears were not genuine and were a form of manipulation. If only he knew how badly I was hurting.

Not only was I hurt by the fact that expressing myself would lead to another divorce reaction, I was shocked by the fact that he called *me* a narcissist. As a therapist, I knew full well what a narcissist looked like. I was also aware of just how much he fit the criteria. I had quietly discovered evidence of his covert narcissistic traits years before. Like many therapists and empaths, I erroneously thought I could repair this. While I never referred to him as a narcissist, I truly believe that Love had caught on to the fact that I was discovering who he really was behind the mask he wore in public. He discovered that I was reading books and articles to educate myself on narcissism and other toxic relationships. After reading a few Google articles himself, he conveniently shifted the blame and convinced himself that I was the problem. Suddenly, all of his character traits were being assigned to me and I was being accused of being the monster that he had shown himself to be throughout the short marriage.

The gentle, soft-spoken man who my family and friends had found Love to be, disappeared again and was replaced by the angry monster who would frequently pop up in our disagreements hurling character attacks, insults and a familiar stink of devaluation. His anniversary roars crushed my spirit as I listened to him express dread about attending the anniversary trip with me. He went on to compare me to a woman who he had dated previously who would have given him sex as soon as they arrived citing my failure to do so.

This way of being had been intermittently sprinkled throughout our marriage. In the beginning, I would go toe-to-toe with him. Over time, this toxic way of being started to wear me down. The little girl who had always been there began to take over for the strong independent woman I once was. I was slowly losing sight of her. I was too exhausted to fight. I even found myself apologizing to him for things I knew full and well I had not done wrong. I just wanted resolution. I became desperate to find a solution and get back on track; desperate to hold the marriage together; desperate for him to love me the way I needed to be loved.

Our marriage seemed to run hot and cold. At first, I didn't know what to call this crazy-making way of being. I just knew it didn't feel right. Once I identified this pattern as a form of abuse, the therapist in me wanted to fix it. Slowly, I began to normalize the abnormal until I didn't know what normal was anymore. I stayed in hopes that things would change and every honeymoon phase strengthened this hope. I hoped that Love would look at his ways and change. I was willing to look at myself so that we could change together. But we could never stay on the same page long enough for that to happen.

"Let's go to therapy," I pleaded with Love. I had already been to therapy and was *still* in therapy trying to learn how to live with the problems in the marriage which were causing me anxiety, depression, and Post Traumatic Stress symptoms.

"I'm not going to therapy," he defied. "You just want too much. I'm tired of trying to prove to you that I love you every day. You are excessive," he blamed.

Excessive? I thought.

I immediately went into self-reflection mode. I reflected over the things I actually *did* want and need from Love; A teammate where there was regular communication and connection, particularly during hard times, and a safe space for emotional vulnerability without fear that they would be used as ammunition. I wanted to be a priority in his life as his wife and to be covered and protected. I had never considered this as excessive until this point. This is where I remembered that people can only be who they are not for so long before they get tired. Love had simply grown tired of pretending to be a husband. He was tired of playing the part of the person he showed me in the beginning.

37

Familiar thoughts resurfaced as I began to question everything I thought I had ever known about the act of love and healthy relationships. *Did I want too much? Was I bad? Why was I not good enough? Maybe I did want too much. Maybe I was overreacting and being too sensitive. Maybe I was to blame for all the trouble in this marriage. Maybe everything he said about me was true. Maybe I was a narcissist. If only I had never cried in Cancun.* These are the self-blaming thoughts that ran through my mind like a train as I was filled with self-doubt.

I later discovered through ongoing individual therapy and research of my own that this form of toxic thinking was common in survivors of emotional, psychological and narcissistic abuse or what mental health professionals call Pathological Love Relationships. I soon discovered that my feelings had been dismissed for so long in the relationship that I had eventually started doing it to myself.

I was emotionally broken as I reflected on how my relationship deal breakers had become workable issues. My dream of a healthy marriage fell apart right before my eyes and my wounds were re-opened. A part of me always knew that I needed to release Love to leave each time he threatened me with divorce. But, I thought I could love the red flags away. Additionally, I didn't want to face divorce and the breakdown of my marriage. If I'm honest the marriage was broken from the start as it was conceived from fear and deceit. I had to release the thought that I could change another person and remember that the only person I could change was myself. The thought of starting over scared me. I was afraid.

"Do it afraid," a voice within me whispered. *"Do it afraid,"* it said again.

And so I did. I eventually freed Love to leave. I let him go, for real this time. It broke my heart but healed my soul. I was now entering the valley of divorce.

Chapter 3
The Shattering

Shatter: To break, to cause to break suddenly and violently into pieces.

He heals the brokenhearted and binds up their wounds
-Psalm 147:3

My fall back to the valley floor sounded like a loud thud as the sharp debris from fear, obligation, guilt and abandonment fell on top of me. I had finally given up on trying to convince Love to work through our marital issues and freed him to leave...but it hurt. I looked around at the familiar valley scenery through a lens of tears, depression, and despair. Thoughts that death would be better filled my mind. Although I never considered suicide, there was a part of me that felt like I was dying as I collected my baggage for the journey through this valley.

I tried my best to keep up my daily routine, but I was only surviving. I went to work each day faking a smile and pretending to be ok. The truth was, I wasn't ok. I couldn't wrap my mind around how someone who said they loved me could stop loving me so quickly. It devastated me. I wore a mask of strength on the outside while inside I was falling apart.

"What are you doing to yourself?" A co-worker jokingly commented on my appearance one day. I had lost a significant amount of weight and conformed to wearing my hair in a simple ponytail every day. The Tiffany that cared about her appearance had slowly faded away. I did all I could to remain at work each day and to not call out all together. I continued to see clients in my private practice, holding space for their pain as I tried to navigate through my own. I cried between sessions and emotionally fell apart each day when I got home just to get up and do it all over again the next day.

"Mama, I can smell your tears again," my daughter Madison said to me one day shortly after Love's divorce announcement. This time I could not hide my tears from her. This time I made no effort to try. In addition to feeling lost and abandoned, I also felt like a horrible mother as my thirteen year old daughter wrapped her arms around me to console me as I wept. I was supposed to be comforting her, not the other way around. Guilt set in as I realized that I had managed to put her in a situation where a man was leaving me and subsequently abandoning her too. She had not even been aware of Love's plans to leave until this point. Once again, I had picked the wrong man; a man who could cut his love on and off again like a light switch allowing it to overflow in good times and snatching it away during the bad.

Love did not immediately move out of the home, which only made things more difficult. He simply moved into the spare bedroom creating a silent and awkward energy throughout the entire home environment. He appeared to go on about his usual day-to-day pattern of living. He wasn't home much and simply resorted to ignoring us when he was. Most of the time it was just Madison and I at home alone. I worried about her seeing me fall apart and into a state of depression. Before this moment, I was Supermom showing her that I could work, go to school, and still be available to her. On this day, all my superpowers were gone. I prayed that I wasn't passing down any of my unhealed wounds to her.

One night, after work as I sat numb on the edge of my bed, Madison entered my room as she commonly did when I got home.

"Hi, Mama," she said sweetly.

"Hey baby" I replied weakly, greeting her with a forced smile.

I watched as she proceeded to my bathroom. Normally, I would have inquired about where she was going and what she was doing but this day I didn't have the energy. I listened as the shower in my bathroom started to run and the shuffling sounds of her Ugg house slippers heading back to me where I remained seated on my bed.

"Take your clothes off and get in the shower, Mama. I'll turn my head so I don't see you naked," Madison instructed as she shuffled to my drawer to retrieve my pajamas.

I didn't want to shower or even change out of my work clothes. I preferred to get in bed with the clothes I had worn that day and simply try again the next day, but I showered for Madison. I knew it would make her feel better and I hoped that it would do the same for me.

I felt weak as I slowly removed my clothes. My limbs felt like bricks as I stepped into the shower and washed my limp body. The drops from the water actually hurt my skin. I wept silently and allowed my tears to disappear into the steam of the shower walls.

Once I got out and dressed in the t-shirt and shorts she prepared for me, Madison dried my week-old Cancun braids with a towel as I sat numb on my bed. She removed the extra-large bonnet from her hair and secured it on my head ensuring that each one of my braids were tightly tucked in. She collected my dirty clothes and disappeared into the kitchen. I sat numb staring at the floor and listened as she rustled around in the kitchen. Minutes later, she returned with a strawberry sour patch yogurt and held it up to my mouth. It was then that I realized I had not eaten in two days.

"Here, Mama. Taste this," she tugged.

I obliged her by taking in a small amount and handed it back to her. She disappeared again into the kitchen this time returning with a piece of leftover tilapia and air fried tater tots on a paper plate.

"Here, Mama. Eat one of my tater tots," she said, holding up a light brown tot to my mouth.

My child was taking on the role of an adult and was clearly trying to get me to eat. I tried, but still ended up rapidly losing 20 lbs.

As I passed through the familiar valley of depression, every day became a goal to survive until the next. Other days it was a goal to survive until the next hour. Some days I didn't think I was going to survive at all. One morning as I stood in the mirror brushing my teeth, I spit into the sink and was met with a sink full of blood. I looked at my frail body in the mirror and cried. My health was beginning to fail from stress and anxiety. "Please help me God," I whispered.

My mind would often shift between missing the man who I met in the beginning of my relationship with Love and accepting the fact that that man really didn't exist. It's been said that a person's true character is revealed not in how they start a relationship; nevertheless, in how they end one. The person I was seeing at the end of my marriage was like a monster who had been hiding under my bed. He had been there all along yet I had refused to believe he was real. I struggled with understanding how he could walk away so abruptly. Sadly, I considered the possibility that he had stopped loving me a long time ago and I had just refused to see it.

The wording in Love's petition for divorce which, I discovered accidentally while trying to clean, was carefully tailored to his advantage and in his best interest, making me feel further exiled. He was requesting that I pay him $24,000 in home equity and revoking any access to medical benefits for Madison and I. Additionally, he requested that I disclaim any interest in his military pension, disability, or retirement benefits despite the fact that he financially benefited from claiming Madison and I in these programs. He even revoked the educational benefit that he had once given to Madison citing that she was not his biological child.

I had never asked Love for any of those things. I had never even seen any substantial fruit or benefit from any of it. Understanding his expectations within our marriage, I had always worked more than one job to make sure Madison and I had what we needed. Even still, the fact that he would go to such efforts to immediately take back the little that he gave was painful.

He cited an old student loan that he had co-signed on as a borrower for me, indicating that he would not be held responsible for it. He further indicated his plans to file separate tax returns from the previous tax year despite the financial benefits due to the both of us for filing jointly. Love showed that he would rather lose money if it meant that there would be any financial benefit to me.

There was even a clause in his divorce documents asking me to agree to forfeit any benefits entitled to me as his wife should he die during the divorce process. I was being treated worse than a stranger without any consideration for me or Madison's well-being. You would have thought I had done something more than cry in Cancun. His cold, callous behavior made this valley of divorce that much harder.

I spent the nights that followed crying myself to sleep and sometimes woke up crying. The sting of his abandonment and deliberate disconnection often woke me up in the middle of the night and the cries continued. On nights when I couldn't cry anymore, I would lay awake thinking back over all that had happened. I would reflect on all the red flags that I either missed or chose to ignore. Sometimes, I would read my journals which documented those instances and others that I chose to hide. But many nights, my mind was consumed with thoughts about Love's ex-wife, Pamela. I thought about something she once said to me before Love and I were married that helped me begin putting all the pieces together.

"Just wait until the real Love comes out" I remembered her warning me in a message. "You are going to see that no trip or gift from him is going to be worth your sanity or peace of mind." Unfortunately, I didn't consider her warning until it was too late.

About a year into the marriage, I accidentally discovered old text communications between him and Pamela in an old cell phone of his that I was planning to clear out for Madison. Looking back, it seemed like I was always accidentally discovering things. Maybe God was trying to warn me. The date on the text messages reflected that this was during a period of marital breakdown prior to their divorce being finalized. In the text, Love was notifying Pamela that he had scheduled for the electricity in the marital home to be shut off despite the fact that she and his child were still living there. Love, it seemed, felt like Pamela was not contributing to the household bills so having the electricity turned off was his play of being the martyr he once told me he would be. Because she was in the *bad box,* her well-being and apparently the well-being of his own child no longer mattered.

"Don't park your car under the garage," he texted with a tone I could only imagine as taunting, vindictive and passive aggressive. "I don't want you to get stuck under there when the lights get shut off today."

I remember her pleading with him in her response as I often did when I was trying to reason with him.

"Please love your child more than you hate me," she responded to his text.

But to no avail. There was no room for problem solving or negotiation. The lights were turned off that day leaving Pamela and their daughter in the dark. These text communications further suggested Love's use of finances as a means of control by withholding money he had previously agreed to give her for their child. He met her desperate requests with a "No" that I could only imagine as being just as dry and cold as he was.

In the same phone, I discovered pictures of medicine bottles for medication often prescribed for anxiety and depression with Pamela's name on them. I saw pictures of a bedroom from multiple angles with plates, cups and piles of laundry in the closet. I recognized the features of the home to be that of the home he previously shared with Pamela. When I asked him about the photos, he became defensive and accused me of starting an argument. In an effort to keep the peace I let it go. It wouldn't be until much later that I would discover Love's true motivation behind the photos.

As I lay in bed at night thinking about Pamela, I recalled how Love had me cluelessly at the house throwing Pamela's things aways, packing up her clothes and putting her belongings out in the garage like this was something they arranged. He immediately had the locks changed and gave me the remote to the garage that, unbeknownst to Pamela, was taken from her car. When Pamela returned to retrieve her belongings, Love called the police and reported that he had an intruder. I imagined the hurt and devastation she must have felt all while thinking that I was purposely colluding with him to hurt her. I thought about the false perception my presence painted of my being involved with Love while they were married. This further deepened our antagonistic relationship and only pitted us against each other.

I reflected on the references of abuse that she would frequently make in her social media posts. I thought about how despite this and her previous warning to me, I had dismissed her as crazy and bitter. I chose to believe Love as he convinced me and others that Pamela was falsely speaking out against him to seek attention, sympathy and to make him look bad. When she spoke out no one took it seriously. Very few people believed her. No one wanted to believe that Love could be that person; especially not me. What I didn't realize then was that I too would one day be on the other side of Love's acts of abuse, twisted facts and false accusations. I too would eventually come to know the cruel man that he could be behind the mask of humility that he wore in public.

There were times during our marriage that I wanted to reach out to Pamela to see if I was crazy or if what I was experiencing was real. I sat with the realization of how Love had managed to recreate the exact same scenario he previously created with Pamela with me. The only difference was that the utility bills were in my name which took away his opportunity to leave Madison and I in the dark. He did, however, have our cell phones turned off which gave me a glimpse of Pamela's experience. Thoughts of Pamela and the flags I chose to ignore often took up my entire night in this valley.

I wept on the drive to see my attorney, Carl. I couldn't believe that just a few weeks prior, Love and I were in Cancun celebrating our anniversary and today I was headed to respond to his petition for a divorce.

"You don't have to give him a damn thing," Carl said loudly in a deep southern drawl after citing all the grounds for divorce in our state. "He doesn't even have grounds! Hell, make him stay married," he continued.

"I don't want to stay married to anyone who doesn't want to be married to me, Carl," I said softly through falling tears. "I just don't want to be put in a bad financial position or have to move because he wants to leave." I ended up looking down at the list of Mississippi grounds for divorce, none of which Love qualified for. Had I been seeking divorce, I could have stood on the commonly used grounds of habitual cruelty. Carl explained that as the defendant in this case, I didn't have the burden of proof. Nevertheless, I was still consumed with sadness and fear as I realized how dark this valley would be.

Seeing my sorrow, Carl got quiet. He propped his foot up on his desk as he leaned back in his fancy lawyer chair in a pregnant pause.

"I know it hurts," he paused again as if he were preparing to say something soft and comforting. "But what you need to do is find the bitch in you, Tiffany!" His voice escalated again magnifying his southern drawl. I wished I knew where she was. I was still in a fog. I was broken and my heart was shattered.

Carl wrote up a response to Love's attorney stating that I would keep the house, have it refinanced but would be keeping any equity citing Love's decision to leave the marriage without cause. Carl also requested $500.00 per month in temporary alimony to help me adjust to a one house-hold income and to obtain new health insurance. I really didn't need or want any money from Love. I never *needed* him financially to survive. But Carl encouraged us to start high. I guess he was just doing what attorneys do.

"Mama, I heard Mr. Love talking loudly in the kitchen today," Madison said to me during a phone call at work a few days later. He still had not moved out. "He said he was not paying you anything. What does that mean?" She asked.

46

Love's response did not surprise me. I found him to be a very stingy man when it came to money, always suspecting someone of trying to "get over on him" so I knew he would fight over every dime. Still, I struggled with the fact that someone who vowed to love and cover us for better or worse was now trying to leave us uncovered. Just the realization that he could be so cold, nasty, and black or white in his thinking of me was devastating. I didn't expect Love to take care of me financially while divorced. If I am honest, he never did that during the marriage. But I certainly didn't expect nor was I going to agree to pay *him* to leave. I did hope he would care for us enough to not deliberately take from us on his way out of the relationship so that he could be comfortable. Unfortunately, this was not the case.

We spent the next 3 months sleeping in our separate rooms fading into strangers who lived under the same roof. Any and all forms of communication went through our attorneys who unsuccessfully tried to negotiate divorce terms which were still to his advantage. My attorney supported and even encouraged me to stand my ground. And so I did. With that, I became Love's adversary, or at least that's how it felt. His cold indifference toward me felt like a punishment and gave me anxiety. I went into a fight, flight or freeze mode each time I heard the sound of the garage opening to indicate his arrival. Love continued to travel and live his life while I continued to work and pick up the pieces to mine.

He would disappear from the house for hours and sometimes even days at a time. When he would make one of his random appearances, he wouldn't even speak to us when he entered a room. I tried not to notice his absence. As time passed it became a welcomed treat when I saw his army bag gone from the closet to indicate that he would not be coming back for a few days. Still, I couldn't help but remember how he was doing the exact same thing when we first met, traveling out of town and spending time at my house while Pamela was at home alone with *their* child. I accepted that arrangement under the belief that they were legally divorced and just waiting to go to court about the property settlement, an arrangement that Love would later ask me to agree to during our divorce process.

I guess I should have known better. I should have been more involved. I should have asked questions. Maybe I was so caught up in what I wanted and getting my happily ever after that I didn't want to know. I wanted the gift of a husband, not realizing that I had picked up a decorated serpent.

Chapter 4
What About Your Friends?

A friend loves at all times,
and a brother is born for adversity.
Proverbs 17:17

It's been said that it is during the worst times of your life that you will get to see the true colors of the people who say they care for you. I believe this to be true. One of the lessons I took away from my last experience in the valley was the value of true friendships and healthy support systems. I fought the urge during my valley of divorce to self-isolate and tried to lean on my network of friendships and supporters. But hard times have a weird way of showing you who your true friends are or at least sorting them out. I found that some people seemed to normalize my experience while others just didn't know how to help, then there were others who just didn't seem to care.

My support circle during the valley of divorce got smaller. The people who I thought would be there for me were absent for one reason or another. They knew my situation but I could count on one hand how many times they had reached out to me to offer support. I tried not to take it personally. I realized that other people had their own lives to live and considered the fact that we were still in the middle of an ongoing global pandemic called COVID-19. But it was a painful realization that some people are simply not going to be available to you when you need them most. I told myself that wherever I was going during that season of my life, those absent people simply could not go. It was also during this valley that I realized just how little people knew and understood about emotional, psychological, and narcissistic abuse, but more on that later.

In a bathrobe and untamed hair, I laid in my bed in a dark room when a friend I had known for years stopped by at my request. I was in no position to help Madison make the Mexican dish she had requested help with that day, so I enlisted the help of this friend. I was almost embarrassed at my weight loss and unkempt appearance when she arrived; nevertheless, I found comfort in knowing that I had known this person for years and would not be judged.

When I found enough strength to leave the darkness of my bedroom, I sat at my kitchen counter fighting back tears as I shared with her the devastation of what I had experienced. She was unresponsive as the tears welled up in my eyes and prepared to roll down my face. It wasn't her silence that troubled me. But her reaction gave me pause.

"Oh my God," she said with a tone of shock. "Are you about to cry?" She asked in surprise standing on the other side of the counter.

I didn't reply. I immediately realized that this wasn't a supportive environment and that this friend was not emotionally available. I stopped my tears from falling and tucked them away for later. After managing to engage in small talk, I went back to the darkness of my bedroom and allowed the tears I had tucked away to finally fall. *Maybe she had never seen me like that and didn't know what to do*, I thought to myself as I lay in the dark. But that was the last time I would hear from that friend.

As I grieved the ending of my marriage or what I had hoped it would be, I also grieved the loss of a very special family friend. This person had been like a father-figure to me and was even a part of my wedding ceremony to Love. He was well aware of my previous valley relationship struggles as well as my struggles in the marriage. He was also the first person I told when I met Love for the first time. I had confided in him about a lot and viewed him as an extension of my family.

Because we all went to church together, I was initially excited when Love and my *father figure* began spending time together. During times of marital trouble, he claimed to have been spending time with Love talking to him about his ways and encouraging him to change and fight for our marriage. Little did I know then that Love was using their time spent together brainwashing him into believing that I was the problem. What I later learned or at least suspected from our later conversations was that my *father-figure* knew of Love's plans to walk away from the marriage at the next sign of trouble. He had simply failed to inform me.

I had discovered, again by accident, that during their time together, Love was plotting and putting my character into question by labeling me with all of his nasty characteristics. This became clear one day when I discovered conversations between them on a public forum I had been following on Narcissistic Abuse. I had been suffering silently for years and there was my *father-figure* exchanging social media posts and joking about the matter as Love projected his nasty ways onto me. I was beyond hurt.

I was not hurt by being called a narcissist by someone like Love. By this point I had recognized this type of behavior as classic projection and a common tactic used by people like him. My hurt came from a place of disappointment in the fact that a person who I considered family, confided in and whom I thought knew me better would take such a casual and indifferent approach to my experience. To add insult to injury, when Love was finally ordered out of the house by a judge, there was my *father-figure* helping Love move. In his normal vindictive manner, Love attempted to deepen my hurt by smiling and loudly taunting using my father-figure's presence as his source of ammunition.

"Aint nothing like family to come through for you during your time of need" he taunted through an evil smirk as my father-figure broke down the bed where I slept and carried it's pieces to the waiting U-haul truck. The guilty look on his face testified against him. Love wanted everything back that he bought or brought into the marriage… and I mean everything. This included the living room and bedroom sets, all the TV's, tables and chairs, and wall hangings. He even took insignificant items like the water hose, buckets, brooms, the toaster, the cutlery set, and the bathroom scale. To my dismay, there was my *father-figure* helping him collect it all.

I watched as Madison anxiously held on to our pet Yorkie, Bella. Had I not been present, I suspect he would have tried to take her too citing that had paid half for her. I tried to assure Madison that no matter what he took, I would not allow him to take Bella. My main interest was the washer and dryer which he also wanted to take but they were ordered to me. Everything else he took was old and would be replaced with upgrades. What hurt most was his intent to leave us with nothing.

While there was a peace that came with Love's final departure from the home, the echo of my cries filled the empty house that night as I thought of my father-figure's position in it all. I cried as I fell asleep on the make-shift bed I created with a single mattress on the floor of my empty bedroom. I replayed his actions over and over in my mind as I experienced the pain of losing a person who I once considered family. I would have traded everything Love took out of the house that day to have my *father-figure* back again. Unfortunately, his choices that day reflected his loyalty and I had to release him from my life too.

While the *quantity* of my supporters decreased, the *quality* of them increased tremendously. I was blessed with divine connections and the right people at just the right time. My good friend and co-worker, Marcus Crowley, who has become like a brother to me was a God sent. He supported me on days that I could not stop crying and spoke life into me when I felt like I was losing myself. He even took Madison to the grocery store on days I could not make it out of bed and picked her up from after school activities when I couldn't. He allowed me the space to grieve and reminded me of my worth as I slowly lost sense of my value. Another friend, Jennifer, came by and took Madison to get food one Sunday. She also sat with me once as I wept in pain. She prayed as she listened to me ask God why through my tears. While I appreciated her presence. I don't think she fully understood how seriously devastated I was during that time. The greeter ministry I was a part of at my church kept me in constant prayer. Their prayers, I am convinced, got me through. My grandmother called almost every day to check in on me and to tell me that she loved me.. Although most days I didn't feel like talking, I appreciated her efforts and concern for me. It was a reminder that I was not alone and if no one else cared about what I was going through, my grandma Minnie did.

Rejed, the ex who I hastily married as a young naive adult, was a listening ear of support and comedic relief. While our hasty marriage ended just six short months after it began, Rejed and I had built a foundation of friendship to fall back on which made it safe to lean to him during my valley. Additionally, Rejed had never been evil or vindictive in his ways the way Love was. Immature, maybe, but Rejed was not toxic nor was he intentional in hurting or taking from me and my child. I welcomed the rebirth of our friendship during that time.

Tashia Gordon prayed for me on days that I could not pray for myself. I will never forget the day she invited me to brunch and said something to me that initiated a change in the way I viewed this valley of divorce.

"What you are going through is bigger than you, Tiffany," she told me. "God is intentional about us and His plans for our lives." I didn't get it then, but I get it now.

While miles away in Chicago, my good friend, Marlon Barber remained a constant voice of reason through my fog of self-doubt and decreasing self-esteem. With a rough and edgy street tone that I absolutely loved, Marlon gave me a man's perspective of it all. He told me that Love was not an accurate representation of a real *man* and that what I wanted was not too much. I was just requesting it from someone who didn't have the capacity to provide.

"The right man would happily give you what you want," he said during one of our many phone conversations. "All you want is unconditional love and communication. Hell, that's free! Don't you become one of those women who let their self-esteem go. You are the Sh_t and you need to know that. Do you hear me?" Marlon would say in his rough-edged urban tone. I enjoyed talking to Marlon and looked forward to our nightly calls. He encouraged me and tried to keep me hopeful, but some days it was still too foggy. I couldn't see what he saw. There was still a part of me that was filled with self-doubt. I kept thinking, *If only I had not cried that day in Cancun. If only I had not expected him to post about our anniversary on social media.* The truth was that there was nothing I could have done at that point to prevent this. Some relationships have an expiration date... others are doomed from the start which I believe was the case for my marriage to Love.

Ironically, Love's ex-wife, Pamela, was a source of initial support. Our paths had finally crossed and I was able to hear her experience with him during their marriage. Pamela's experiences with Love were eerily very similar to mine. Familiar periods of verbal abuse, devaluation, character attacks, and an eventual abandonment of the marriage had played out in her world similar to the way things were unfolding in mine.

My relationship with Pamela introduced me to the truth about what really went on during their divorce process, or at least things that Love had hidden from me. Love had initiated a divorce from her on the grounds of habitual cruelty which were based on lies and twisted truths. Attempts to demolish her character in court were made by suggesting that she also had a substance abuse problem. The pictures of the depression and anxiety medication bottles I had previously discovered were used against her in court to bring her mental stability into question. This was followed up with Love's attempt to weaponize her help-seeking in the form of therapy for symptoms that he likely contributed to. The pictures of the bedroom with plates, cups and piles of laundry were also used by Love and his attorney as ammunition to further kill her character as a wife, mother and as a person. As the saying goes, a leopard never changes his spots. I considered this quote as I later sat with the realization that Love had used the same dirty plays on me.

While Pamela and I initially connected through common experiences with Love, we also connected on what I had believed to be a true friendship.

While we had very similar experiences with Love, one difference I noted between us was our responses to Love's ways. While his cold and disconnected responses debilitated me, Pamela grew numb to them and eventually became indifferent to him all together. Oh how I longed to experience that feeling of indifference. But hearing Pamela's experience with Love and seeing that she had survived gave me hope that I could too. Pamela would call to check on me each day and would send motivational quotes to keep me going.

"Keep pushing," she would say. "You are stronger than you think." One day she presented me with a bracelet that was inscribed on the inside to read "keep f_cking pushing." I welcomed her support during that time.

I tried my best not to become a burden or be overly reliant on people. I only shared my vulnerabilities with the ones who seemed to care; those who were concerned about why I was distant instead of getting offended by the fact that I was. I was sad that the people I thought would be there were not, but I was grateful for the few people who were. In the end, there was a sobering awareness that no matter how supportive people were or tried to be, the healing work was mine and mine alone.

Chapter 5
Dear God It's Me Again

Before they call I will answer.
While they are yet speaking, I will hear.
Psalms 91:15

O f all my supports, the one that remained eternally present through this valley and others had been my heavenly Father, even during times when I could not feel Him near. But, what do you say to God when your pain leaves you speechless, again? Sometimes *God help me* was the only thing I could utter. What do you do when the pain of a valley still doesn't go away? You cry. You weep. You moan in pain. You sleep in the dark to the sounds of motivational sermons from YouTube and hope something happens in the night that makes you feel better. You read. You write. You ask others to pray for you until you can pray for yourself. I had been in this place before, though not to this extent, and I was back again asking God for help. *Dear God, it's me again.*

I leaned heavily on my faith during this time. *"God help me"* were sometimes the only three words I could muster up enough strength to say some mornings when I opened my eyes. Some days I hated that the sun came up. The familiar feeling of bricks being sealed to my feet came back as I struggled to get out of bed and on my knees to pray. Each day when the alarm sounded for work, I woke up to the sobering awareness that my marriage had come to an end on the anniversary of the day it began.

As I continued to work and deteriorate physically and emotionally, I often wondered how and why God would allow this.

"How could you let him do this to me, Lord?" I would question God. "Why God? Why?" I cried out in a familiar valley scream. My prayers vacillated between asking God to save my marriage and praying for peace and strength to get through the day without breaking. As Loves' distance toward me became colder, my prayers for God to save my marriage changed to prayers that God would soften Love's heart. I prayed that He would give Love new eyes to see me and to see that I was not this horrible person that he had conveniently convinced himself I was. Although Love treated me like a stranger, a part of me still wanted to make peace with him, even if we were not going to be together.

I began missing church and was no longer active in service as I had previously been before. I was too physically and emotionally fragile to be there in person. I didn't want the questions and I was embarrassed at the fact that I had chosen wrong again. Additionally, I didn't want to risk breaking down emotionally, so I stayed away from church. At least if I was at home, I could break down privately.

While I stopped attending church in-person, I continued to attend church virtually at home in my living room via our church's live stream. The COVID-19 pandemic had created a platform for that. Even then, it felt like a sacrifice. Some mornings I would cry through the entire praise and worship portion. I would try my best to listen to the message, listening for something, anything that was for me and my situation. But my mind kept going back to what had happened, how it happened, how easily it happened, and the fact that I didn't know what was going to happen.

"Dear God, it's me again. Please help me!" I would say every morning when I opened my eyes and multiple times throughout the day.

"Why are you allowing this, God?" I questioned Him some nights as I lay in a fetal position crying. I questioned God as to why He would allow Love to get away with doing this-again. I could not believe the length he was going. He demonstrated just how dirty and vengeful he was behind that mask of soft-spokenness. He had walked away from his previous marriage. Now he had walked away from ours leaving me devastated.

"Why God? Why? Have I not been through enough?"

Many times, God was quiet. I wanted to get angry with God and stop talking to Him as I had done before. But I knew doing this was a mistake. I would surely die. I didn't have any more options. I had to stick with God. I was at rock bottom.

"I just know that God is going to take care of it," Madison said to me one day as we sat outside talking. Where was my faith? How did this child have more faith than me? My heart ached even more.

With time, my three-word prayer eventually got a little longer. When my emotions prevented me from praying from my heart, I would just say God's word. I had been a member of Faith for Life Church for the last thirteen years which is a WORD teaching church. If ever I didn't know what to pray, I knew I had been taught to pray the word of God. Sometimes emotional pain makes it difficult to recall scripture we know so well. That was definitely the case for me. But I was able to remember the scripture that states, "One would chase a thousand and two would chase ten thousand" (Psalm 133:1). With that, I began including Madison in my prayer sessions. We both got up and prayed each day. We even prayed for Love for a period of time. I was also taught to use my spiritual weapon in my arsenal of praying in the Spirit. So, that's what I did. It was not always easy. Many days I simply didn't feel like praying.

"Faith is not a feeling," I could almost hear my Bishop saying. Just like marriage is not based on a feeling, neither was faith. So, just like in my marriage, I did what I did not feel like doing…I prayed.

Over time, I eventually got to the point where I was able to wake up each day and read from a devotional book. I had hoped that the words would heal me and give me enough strength to push through the day. For some reason, though, it seemed like it took me forever to read and absorb a single passage. Small passages soon turned into larger passages and eventually I developed a desire to read throughout the day. I immersed myself in study. I tried to stick close to the word and began to speak it daily even though many times I felt absolutely nothing. I had nothing left but my faith and many days even that was shaky. I would often go back and forth in my mind during that time about whether or not God was going to show up for me. Still, there was a lingering question about why God had not saved my marriage.

One day, after a period of what felt like silence from God, I felt an urge in my spirit to read back over my journal entries which documented the previous five years of my marriage to Love, *"and take a highlighter,"* I heard the Spirit say. God's voice became clearer as I read over the yellowed highlighted events of my marriage which reflected a pattern of emotional, psychological, and three different episodes of physical abuse. I cried as I read and recalled the time Love pulled a gun out of his pocket and threatened to "blow my brains out." I cried more as I realized how my boundaries had crumbled and recalled my mother's response after telling her about this event.

"Tiffany, that should have been the end right there. But only you know when enough is enough," she said as I cried on the phone to her that day.

It was then that I realized two things: First, God had never told me to marry Love. In haste, I had made the decision to marry him, and then expected God to co-sign on it. I wanted my happily ever after so badly that I was willing to overlook red flags and not consult God. Secondly, while in the marriage, God had instructed me to release Love multiple times, but I was disobedient. I was afraid to let the marriage go. I didn't want to start over. I wanted to repair what was never mine…and so I suffered. This was a sobering awareness. Yet, the words of J.I Packer brought me comfort: "Our God is a God who not merely restores, but takes up our mistakes and follies into his plan for us and brings good of them."

Additionally, I went back and read my first book to pick up previous lessons in the valley and to remind myself of what I had told other people. I had to take my own medicine and it was not always sweet. One night shortly after my fall back to the valley floor, I was scheduled to do an online interview with a local author. I really did not feel up to it as I was emotionally drained, but I felt obligated as it had been scheduled well before I entered divorce valley. So I did it. "Give me something to say Lord," I whispered before putting on a fake smile to start the show.

The interview went well. Towards the end as I discussed and promoted my first book, I felt led to share something with the audience.

"As an author, anytime you are brave enough to publish a book instructing others on how to live through and overcome adversity, life will eventually present you with a personal opportunity to prove just how much you believe about the words you wrote. Several weeks after I released this book," I continued, holding up the book, "I got my opportunity and I am still going through it right now."

I was suddenly overcome with emotion. Tears began to fall from my face as I watched my nose turn red in the camera. I was so overcome with emotion that I could not go on speaking. I watched as women from all over the platform began to comment, agree, like, and share the video. When I regained my composure, I added a message of hope by declaring that before this time next year, I would be back on the show with a testimony. I later received an outpouring of love, prayers, and support from women who I didn't even know. I happily welcomed it.

"You might as well go on and shout now," I remember one of the viewers saying. I had no idea of the supernatural manifestation from God that was about to come my way. While my mind was unable to see beyond the darkness of this valley, my heart held on to God's word. It was at that time that I decided to tell my story.

As I spoke with God on a deeper level, I began to reevaluate my motivation for sharing my story. I consulted God to ensure that I was doing it with the right spirit and not from a vindictive place. I wanted to make sure that my hands and heart were clean before Him. My goal was and still is to bring awareness to the impact of toxic relationship patterns, eradicate our tendency to normalize these patterns, and to show people that God can and will protect and deliver those that belong to Him. Sharing my story is now part of that mission, my healing and what I've come to believe as God's platform for me as a healed helper in my profession.

Additionally, according to Ephesians 5:11, "We are not to participate in unfruitful deeds of darkness but rather expose them." I kept quiet about my experiences in my marriage out of fear, obligation, and guilt as well as the misbelief that I could fix it. Shame also kept me there in addition to the belief that God didn't want me to divorce. That is when 1 Corinthians 7:15 came back to my mind which reads, "But if an unbeliever leaves, let it be so. The brother or sister is not bound in such circumstances. God calls us to live in peace." Additionally, I knew that God did not want a daughter of His in an unfruitful marriage. Jesus himself cursed a fig tree for failing to be fruitful (Mark 11:12-25).

An additional lesson I discovered was that failing to expose the darkness of abuse will keep others in bondage to it. Abuse does not always have to be physical. In fact, it's the lasting impact of emotional and psychological abuse that is the most devastating. I had finally understood my assignment. Not only would my story bring people to God, it would also help others see that no one is immune from the inevitable harm that comes from being in a relationship with toxic personalities…not even me. These lessons would take me into the next level of seeing the devil face-to-face.

Chapter 6
Off Comes the Devil's Mask

For our struggle is not against flesh and blood, but against the rulers, against the authorities, against the powers of this dark world and against the spiritual forces of evil in the heavenly realms.
–Ephesians 6:11

Sometimes the devil comes wearing sheep's clothing but behind the mask he is calculating, vindictive, and vile. As a believer, I knew that Satan was and had always been a destroyer and an accuser (Revelations 12:10). His aim is to shatter spirits, hurl accusations, half-truths, and insults. He needs to confuse and devastate. But he also needs a human body to do it.

"My client is 100% disabled and on a fixed income. He is unable to work. His disability benefits are his only source of income. Tiffany, on the other hand, has a full-time job as a therapist. She also has a private practice where she works as a counselor. Additionally, my client tells me that she wrote a book which she has on Amazon for $20 per copy."

My heart pounded as I read over the new negotiation responses from Love's attorney to mine. He was now requesting alimony from me. I had come to know that Love was money hungry and financially stingy, considering that financially, we lived like roommates. Sadly, this was a brand new low, even for him. I had spent the entire marriage working two jobs, writing a book, picking up contract work, and trying to make something of myself while he stayed home relaxing. Now here he was malingering to his financial advantage.

I recalled how in the beginning of our courtship Love had put me on a pedestal for my strong work ethic as he compared and pitted me against his ex-wife for not doing the same. Suddenly, the rules of the game had changed. Now, the very trait that he found attractive about me in the beginning was being weaponized to support his financial greed. He was divorcing me, revoking medical insurance for me and Madison in the middle of a pandemic while also requesting alimony and to be paid 24,000 worth of equity in our home. To agree to this would be a win-win for him.

Reading those words from Love's attorney hit me like a ton of bricks. In a panic, I called my attorney who encouraged me not to panic, but it was too late. A combination of hurt and anger filled my body. I had always known that Love was trying to beat the system, and while I was turned off by his lack of ambition and vision, I never thought he would stoop this low to use me to increase his comfort in the world. The devil's mask was disintegrating right in front of me. I had seen glimpses of this devil before, but it was always followed up with some random act of kindness that made me doubt and at times even forget the evil I had seen. This time it was different. *God help me!* I began to repeat again.

I immediately began my search to prove that Love was lying about his income. I started searching through drawers and old boxes. I was looking for something, anything to prove that he had more income than what he claimed and that he could take care of himself. My search would yield documents reflecting benefits of well over 6,000 a month. While that may not seem like much to some people, that is certainly a lot for the position as a house husband. Meanwhile, I was out working 10 hour days and being punished for coming home tired or not in the best of moods some days.

Eventually, I noticed that pieces of my personal mail would come up missing as I made correspondence with my attorney and financial institutions. I knew Love stayed home each day while I went to work guarding the mailbox like Mr. from the Color Purple. I didn't worry much about it though. I had seen all I needed to see. But, one piece of evidence I ran across shed a new light on exactly the type of person I was dealing with.

I discovered old documents that made me lose total respect for Love as a person. I had already lost respect for him as a man for trying to take advantage of my work ethic so that he could stay home with the coffee maker. But, I lost total respect for him as a person when I discovered what he had done next. As I continued to read through documents and records, I discovered that he had used the death of Madison's father as a *recent death event* contributing to his distress and subsequent *need* for increased financial support. I was angry that he would even speak about my daughter's deceased father, especially since he never knew him and considering the fact that he had left me stranded at the hospital the night he died. Love's behavior showed me that not only was he an opportunist, but he was also self-seeking.

I refused to agree to his terms for divorce. Love was free to leave the marriage but I refused to pay him a dime to do so. So, he upped his game. He threatened to take interest in a home that I purchased when I was 26, well before I met him. I had kept the home as a rental property and was using the rent payments to pay Love my half of the mortgage on our marital home. Love had always held me responsible for his decision to sell his old marital home and was angry that I didn't sell mine. He also threatened to take an interest in my counseling business supported by the lie that he had helped me start it. Additionally, Love was threatening to hold me responsible for the purchase of the brand new vehicle that he purchased without my knowing citing it as marital debt. I found myself sad again asking myself why he was doing this. Then I remembered what he had done to Pamela and who he was. This sobered me up again to who I was dealing with and motivated me to fight back.

New information about Love kept coming and I eventually learned that his predator ways had extended beyond me. I found out about another woman, who shall remain nameless, who he was seeing two months before he pursued me and this woman came with receipts. She too had been pursued by Love in her social media inbox. The content of his messages demonstrated the mirroring nature of a predator. From her hair right down to her music likes, he had been watching before gaining enough confidence to approach her.

May 8th 10:06 pm (Facebook inbox of another woman)

Love: I apologize for coming in your inbox, but I must say, u have a uniqueness that I have never seen

May 10th 7:32pm

Her: No need to apologize. Thank you very much

May 13th 6:28pm

Love: You too young to listen to so much old school

May 13 6:51pm

Her: Oh really, lol

Love: Definitely. Being that u are a 90s baby

May 13th 7:11 pm

Her: Thanks, but I'm an 80s baby

Love: I see you take good care of yourself. Thought you were about 25

Her: Aww thank you

Love: You're welcome. Hopefully I can catch you out one day and maybe u might let me buy you a drink

Her: Sure. A glass of wine will be fine

Love: Cool. You look like a cabernet or merlot young lady. What do you drink?

May 14th 11:44am

Her: Both

Love: Would you like to have my number so u can let me know when I can get you that drink?

Her: Are you single though?

Love: I have been going through a divorce since 2012 which will be finalized on June 1. But I have been single for almost 3 years. Here is my number.

They eventually went out on a dinner date. According to this woman, Love spent the entire evening talking about how horrible of a person his soon to be ex-wife was. He even pulled out this cell phone to show her pictures of the piles of laundry, bedroom chaos and medication bottles that I would later discover. According to her, because of his actions, she never saw him again. She knew that if he would do that to another woman, he would certainly do the same things to her.

May 16th 3:49pm

Love: I was thinking about you. Your hair is laid!

Her: ……….. (No reply)

She had curved him. In doing so, she was also able to dodge the dirty bullet that would later strike me. Oh, how I wished that I had dodged that dirty bullet. I recalled Love casually mentioning his brief encounter with this woman during our courtship. He conveniently left out the part about his actions and referred to her as crazy. He also made it seem as if this woman had been chasing him down for a relationship and that she had expressed upset about his getting engaged to me. The receipts determined that was a lie. Love's mask continued to dissolve revealing his true mission, character and nature.

Eventually, I was formally served with divorce papers on my job even though Love and I were still living in the same house at that time. I recalled how Pamela was served with divorce papers on a random day while they were at home together watching TV. Being served with divorce papers at my place of employment was a humiliating experience. But I knew that this was Love's intent.

This new set of documents contained accusations of cruel and habitual treatment, allegations of a substance abuse problem and littered with language which made his recent Google search on Narcissistic terms and abuse patterns obvious. Pictures of year old medication bottles containing pain medication prescribed to me following a fibroid surgery would be used to support Love's accusations that I abused opioids. Pictures he took of full medication bottles containing anti-depressant and anxiety medication prescribed to me during the marriage would also be used to bring my mental stability into question. I was amused but not surprised at how easily he could twist and manipulate the reality of things to fit his agenda.

As if reading from the same set of playbook tactics, Love used my emotional reactions to his abuse, things shared with him in confidence and my periods of depression as a result of marital conflict to further support his claims of mental instability. Following his vacation kick, I entered therapy on my own to deal with the emotional aftermath. For normal human beings, this might be viewed as healthy and even commendable. But for toxic personalities, such help-seeking behavior is often weaponized and viewed as ammunition to win. Love had my therapy records subpoenaed in hopes to discover something to support his claims. While nothing in my records supported his claims of my character, his playbook tactics certainly solidified the truthfulness of his.

We eventually went to court for a temporary hearing. Waking with a strut of confidence I had never seen before, Love approached the witness stand prepared to attack. He raised his hand and swore to tell the truth, the whole truth and nothing but the truth before arrogantly taking his seat. I listened as he cited concerns for his personal safety as a result of my alleged mental instability. I found this humorous and suppressed the urge to laugh. The same man who had kicked me down in anger, pulled a gun on me and would curse me out like a stranger was now reporting that *he* was afraid of *me*. I also found his safety concerns ridiculous considering the fact that up until that point, he had still refused to move out of the house.

Love didn't get very far in his antics. My attorney immediately objected citing the purpose of the temporary hearing. We were there to determine who would live in the house until the final divorce trial. Love would have to delay his lies, accusations and character attacks until the final trial. I suspected that he would wait with baited breath.

That initial urge that I had to laugh faded to disappointment as Love continued his testimony regarding his desired living arrangements. I listened as he tried to convince the judge that Madison and I needed to be ordered out of the home because he was disabled, couldn't work and had nowhere to go. It was a marvelous act, but the judge didn't bite. Love was given 30 days to move out of the house. For a moment, I felt a sense of relief. I would no longer have to experience the awkward interaction of living under the same roof with someone who didn't even speak when he walked in the room. I would no longer be startled by the sudden opening and closing of the doors to the home which was often my only indication that Love was in the house. I found relief in the thought that Madison and I could finally start to live somewhat of a normal life; consequently, my relief was short lived.

Sitting in my car after I pulled into my garage that day, tears began to fall as the reality of things again set in. Even though I had been awarded temporary possession of the house, the relief that initially came with it had vanished. For some reason, I still felt crushed in spirit and defeated. I still couldn't believe this was happening. I wrestled with the thought that he would try to have me and my child put out of the house for his own benefit. My prayers went back to my three-word default prayer. *God help me!* I cried silently as I thought of all that was happening in this valley. I thought about Madison and how this was affecting her.

As the tears fell, my cries were given a sound that turned into screams, loud penetrating screams that echoed throughout my garage where I remained parked with my car ignition running. After reaching an emotional climax of grief, I slowly allowed those screams to turn to surrender to God and from surrender into worship. I exited my car and fell to my knees. My hands were raised as the echo of my sobs bounced through my garage. My worship then turned to praise as I found the strength to stand to my feet again. In a sudden urge of sacrificial praise, I ran around my garage, dancing, clapping, skipping and praising God to the gospel music which played from my running car. This may have looked totally insane to an outside watcher, but I had to do something to get back in the faith fight. The devil had removed his mask and things would get worse before they got better.

This is the year of winning and victory! This was the word delivered by Bishop Butler during New Year's Eve service at the beginning of that year. There were a series of church sermons that followed later which focused on contending with the enemy for this victory. I didn't realize it at the time, but that year would not only be a year of contending with the enemy for my victory, it would also be a year of contending for my faith. My faith would be tested and retested and I would find myself vacillating between faith and fear. The only solution was to get out of my emotions, pick up my spiritual weapons, and fight. It was time to contend.

Remembering that my struggle was not against flesh and blood, I stopped trying to fight Love in the way he was fighting me. I knew that I could not fight that type of evil with the world's weapons. Instead, I decided to fight him on my knees through prayer. The more his mask fell and his true nature was revealed the more I came to recognize my circumstances as a spiritual warfare.

I started off praying for Love and covering him in prayer even though he had left me and my child uncovered on so many levels. Over time, I felt the nudge in my spirit that I was supposed to stop praying for him. So, I did just that. I stopped. My prayers then became rebuking prayers to scatter, route, and confuse the enemy I had come to recognize. I prayed against that evil spirit in Love because that spirit was still in my house at this point. I find it no coincidence that as my prayers progressed, I saw less and less of Love or any evidence of his presence. He eventually moved out earlier than ordered and it was a welcomed relief.

As my prayers continued to change, so did I. I would have my occasional moments of sadness, but my tears were drying up and my heart was healing. God had allowed me to see enough to confirm that I no longer wanted to be married to him either. But I most certainly was not going to pay him to leave. While there was still healing work that I needed to do, I eventually began to see myself with the strength to start my life over, happy and without him. It felt good. This was the beginning of my awakening.

Chapter 7
The Awakening

The truth will set you free.
John 8:31

While Love's announcement for divorce initially crippled me emotionally, the final slip of his mask made it much easier to release him along with any emotions tied to him. I came to accept that the person I found him to be in the end was who he had always been. It was during this time that I also began to experience an awakening on multiple levels. My educational and spiritual awakening was initiated as I dove into research about the abuse that no one talks about…the emotional and psychological abuse that often comes along with pathological love relationships with narcissistic personalities. It was during this time that I ran across a page from a lady by the name of Shannon Savoy. Not only was she a survivor of narcissistic abuse, she was also a Christian and someone who taught on narcissism from a spiritual perspective.

"I don't diagnose, but I can discern," she would say.

Before discovering Shannon, I was operating from what I knew about narcissism from a purely clinical perspective. I discovered that the evils described in narcissism can even be found in the descriptions of these spirits throughout scripture. I began to compare what I was learning about clinical narcissism to the word of God. As I continued to follow Shannon, I was exposed to an entire community of others whose stories sounded exactly like mine. I could not believe that there were others who had experienced the exact same tactics that I had experienced with Love. For the first time,

I had the language to identify what I had experienced and a name to call it. I no longer felt crazy.

This may sound radical to some, but I also received revelation about the mission behind my entire marriage to Love. I pray that you chew the hay and spit the sticks. What I learned through this period of awakening through prayer and revelation from God was that I had married Love thinking he was my soul mate when in actuality, he represented my demonic assignment. I am convinced that my marriage to him was a demonic attack sent to destroy me. Not only was it sent to destroy me, it was also sent to destroy my seed, my daughter. Just as God is in the business of generational blessings, the enemy is in the business of generational curses. The sins of the parents often fall on the children leaving them susceptible to similar experiences of emotional devastation and cycles of woundedness. Just the thought of my daughter marrying someone like Love frightened me. This motivated me to learn more so that I could teach my daughter and others.

As I continued my awakening, I had to reexamine my old emotional injuries to assess for cracks and places that did not heal properly. I also began to remember dreams that I previously stored away remembering that God also speaks to us that way. Months before I met Love, I had a dream that I was getting married. I remember being overjoyed with excitement as I stood at the altar in all white in front of a tall man who also wore white. But what stood out the most in this dream was the fact that I could not see this man's face; it was hidden from me.

I believed this dream to be a manifestation of what was coming to me; however, in haste, I failed to consider God's timing. So, when Love showed up shortly after that dream, I erroneously took the counterfeit husband instead of the one God had promised me. Like Abraham did with Hagar, sometimes our decision to manufacture our own destiny gets us out of the will of God and causes us to suffer. I sometimes wonder if God stopped showing me things to come so soon because he knew I would get too excited and mess up His plans.

I had to repent before God for seeking my own way and failing to seek Him before choosing to marry Love. I was so caught up in his pseudo kindness and my own desires for that happily ever-after that I failed to take the time to hear from God. I jumped into a marriage with a man whose true character I really didn't know and in doing so made a covenant with a demon spirit. Even when God gave me signs, I ignored them along with my internal alarms that told me he was not the man in my dream. Repenting was my acknowledgement to God that I had missed Him and my willingness to do it His way next time.

An additional level of my awakening involved me telling myself the truth about the marriage and why I held on to it so tightly. The truth was that I had allowed dysfunction to go on for so long that I lost the courage to do what I *knew* needed to be done before I was *forced* to do it. I was emotionally irresponsible and suffered as a result. Even still, I realized that there was a grieving process associated with the loss of a relationship, even the toxic and dysfunctional ones. Reflecting on my emotional fall back to the valley floor at the beginning, I realized that I was grieving the death of a relationship that had never really been born. I was grieving the loss of what I had hoped the marriage would be. I eventually had to let the husband I manufactured in my dreams die. I accepted that Love was who he was and that his character was not a reflection of me. Acknowledgement of these issues was part of my awakening which eventually led to my healing.

During my awakening, I also got clear on exactly what I wanted from a man so that my prayers to God could be more specific and my boundaries were established. After so many relationship failures, most people would have given up. But not me. I wanted what God promised me and I was willing to wait and do it His way this time. During my marriage to Love, I had convinced myself that it was not ok to want what I wanted. So, I settled hoping that one day he would love me in the way I wanted to be loved. But the reality is that people cannot give you what is not inside of them to give. It doesn't make them bad people, it just means they are not a good fit for you. I also recalled Queen Mother Iyanla Vanzant's infamous statement where she says, "We don't get to tell people how to love us. We get to see how they love and decide if we want to participate."

My new revelations empowered me; they comforted me. They gave me hope and a sense of relief when the internalization of Love's actions towards me started to creep in. Love made a decision to leave the marriage. For him and others like him, they have free-will to do so. TD Jakes spoke to this so eloquently when he said, "People leave you because they are not joined to you and if they are not joined to you, you can get super glue and you can't make them stay. LET THEM GO."

The lesson here is this: Some people simply are not emotionally invested in us which makes it easy for them to walk away. Trying to hold them together with glue only makes a mess. This also speaks to the importance of knowing your personal attachment style and intimacy needs. A relationship between an avoidant and anxious attachment styles can be very difficult, particularly when one or both are not able or willing to do the work. My journey of awakening was sobering but was healing. Healing, as I have learned, is not always linear. Sometimes it's spiral, winding and gradual. But one thing healing will always be is continuous.

Chapter 8
Trial Day: When God Shows Up

The wicked lay in wait for the righteous, intent on putting them to death but the Lord will not leave them in the power of the wicked or let them be condemned when brought to trial

Psalm 37:32-33

*Do not be afraid of them
for I am with you and I will rescue you.*

Jeremiah 1:8

They will fight against you but will not overcome you, for I am with you.

Jeremiah 1:19

Sometimes, you must allow people to take you all the way to the cross in order for the work to be finished. Even the people who betray you are part of the plan. Jesus could not have completed the finished works without Judas. The scriptures at the beginning of this chapter are some of the scriptures that I stood on throughout my divorce process and right up until the day of the trial. I carried these scriptures in my heart as I arrived at court for the final divorce hearing or what I call the grand finale.

Days leading up to the hearing, I found myself with mixed emotions. I thought about the fact that a man who once promised to love and protect me now acted with such malice by trying to put me to an open shame with lies. I was back on trial with him except that this time it would be public record instead of the private blaming Love did behind closed doors. Nevertheless,

I was ready for whatever he was coming with. I was ready to contend and chose to believe that God would vindicate me.

"God is intentional about us," I heard my friend Tashia say in my mind. I kept this in mind as I arrived at court. I knew that if God did not show up for me no one could.

On the day of the hearing, I arrived at the courthouse alone. While I was anxious and alone physically, I knew there were invisible forces there on my behalf. Love arrived with his sister and a cousin of his who were there to testify against me. I found that odd considering I had never spent any significant amount of time with either of them and neither of them had ever been present during marital conflict. I realized that these were Satan's secretaries. Recalling what I had learned about the narcissistic family system, I also recognized their positions as the flying monkeys who blindly support abusers and do their bidding.

Sitting alone, I watched as four familiar police officers entered the courtroom hallway. I recognized them as the officers who responded to my 911 call during a domestic altercation before Love moved out. They had been subpoenaed to testify on Love's behalf. Although there was absolutely nothing in the police report to substantiate any wrongdoing on my part, Love enjoyed the drama of it all and was coming with whatever he could to bring a case against me.

In preparation for trial, Love created a thumb drive of photos and text messages to support his claims of my mental instability, habitual cruelty and substance abuse which I was allowed to view before the final hearing. Added to his list of accusations was a new allegation of adultery. Love had added this after seeing me at a football game in Memphis where he reportedly spent the entire weekend running around the city collecting evidence. This was also evident by the blurry photos he attempted to capture of me talking to a man in the lobby of the hotel and supposedly walking toward the elevator with him. Finalizing his list of accusations was my failure to act with reciprocity by buying juice for his sister after her illness and claims that I mistreated his daughter by failing to invite her to Madison's 10th birthday party. I again suppressed the urge to laugh as I read over his petty pretrial testimony for which we were to take up a full day in court.

My urge to laugh weakened when I saw pictures of him and Madison together taken at different points throughout the marriage. The photos were to serve as evidence that he was a great father to Madison and further support his *good guy* act. I wondered if he had considered Madison the day he finally decided to move out of the house following the temporary hearing. Given 30 days to move out, he was to notify me of the move date so that proper arrangements could be made to have Madison out of the house and have someone there on my behalf to ensure a peaceful transition. But, communicating like an adult was not Love's strong suit and the transaction that day was anything but peaceful. Love chose to show up one day unannounced with a group of men and began removing things from the home. Madison, who was sleeping in the next room, was home alone, scared and clueless. I recalled the fear in her voice the day she called me at work.

"Mama, some men are in the house taking stuff out," she cried.

I was at work 18 miles away and could not get to her fast enough to settle my fears. So, I called the police to go over to the house as I raced home. The four officers subpoenaed for court met me there. In Love's mind, my actions of calling the police that day constituted cruel and habitual treatment which entitled him to a divorce, alimony and $24,000. He seemed to work harder to get out of the marriage than he did to save it.

As a typical practice, my attorney met with me before the hearing for some final discussions. I had no intention of settling with Love under his terms and was ready to go to trial. We were at the cross and I was willing to let him take me all the way. My ego kicked in as I told myself that Love may have availed in his playbook pattern of lies before but he wasn't going to get away with it with me. If I was truly this drug abusing, abusive, cheating wife who he had painted me out to be, then I was going to make him prove it and pay for it. It was show time.

My attorney informed me that he and Love's attorney had been in communication with the judge in pretrial discussion a few days before. He had even spoken with the judge a few hours prior to the start of the hearing. To my surprise, after reading over the complaint, the judge was encouraging us to settle this matter out of court and that there would be no hearing. I could only conclude that he simply did not want to waste an entire day nor the court's time with Love's frivolous accusations which took up 30 pages of court documents. Once again, Love's presentation of lies and character attacks would be placed on hold.

After Carl was done speaking, I sat with the information. That's when I heard God say, "Let it go. I got the rest."

I tried to put my ego to the side and listen to the voice again. "Let it go. He will not put you to an open shame and I will give you back double for your trouble," I heard God's voice again.

I considered the fact that I wanted a divorce from Love just as badly as he wanted one from me. While I still refused to pay this grown man alimony or give him financial support, I did soften a little and was willing to be advised by my attorney regarding equitable figures that were comfortable for *me* and put that on the table. The tables had suddenly turned and the negotiations were now in my favor. The judge was also in support of my offer. But, in his normal argumentative way, Love argued over an extra 2000 dollars and the 90 days that the judge had already granted me to refinance the house. He wanted to go to trial. He wanted to win. I sat quietly in the witness room and listened to his hallway tantrum.

"Man that's Bull shit!!" Things were not getting his way. He was still unsatisfied, but the case had been closed. I listened as all of the witnesses who Love had arrived with were sent home, their shoes sounding as they walked down the court stairs and out the building. No one was going to be able to help Love lie today. The thumb drive he hoped to use would never be opened and I would not have to say a word to defend myself against his lies.

The final ending of my marriage to Love was a mix of emotions between feeling pure joy and feeling absolutely nothing. I signed the divorce papers happily and walked out of that courthouse into my destiny. It wasn't until I got home that I realized how Isaiah 54:17 had played out right before my eyes that day.

"No weapon formed against you shall prosper and every tongue that rises against you will be SILENCED." The lying tongues were indeed silenced that day." Glory be to God!

I eventually refinanced the house with my name solely on the title and the deed. I got a great interest rate, a comfortable mortgage, paid off my car, received a large refund from the mortgage company and was left with 100k in equity in my home. God gave me back double for everything that the enemy tried to steal. I felt like a winner. I felt free!

I thought about how the word received from the Lord the year before, "This is your year of winning and victory" had masterfully worked out in my life. After all I had been through, I could finally see clearly again. The dark cloud that hung over my head was gone. I had come out of the fire yet, I didn't even smell like smoke. It was finally over! To God be the glory!

Chapter 9
Blended Family Problems

O f the many and often frivolous arguments that came up in my marriage to Love, one ongoing issue was the difficulty we experienced with the blending of our families. This was also the topic that came up most frequently in many of our unsettled arguments. As I read through his divorce responses, it was clear that 90% of his complaint for divorce rested on accusations that I somehow mistreated his youngest daughter. Love was totally convinced of this in his deranged way of thinking that he simply lacked the ability to see things outside of it.

I felt that this topic of blended family issues was worth discussion as part of this book and was deserving of a chapter of its own for multiple reasons. First, I recognize that this issue was indeed a valid challenge that requires work in any blended family and particularly while married to Love. However, I am also convinced that common difficulties in this area were magnified and twisted to pollute his already tainted view of me to justify his abandoning the marriage.

Love had two daughters; however, it always appeared as though he mostly took issue with me when it came to his youngest one, who we will call Samantha. Madison and Samantha were ages seven and eight when Love and I were married. In the beginning, the blending of our families seemed to be going normal, despite the manageable tensions that were present between Pamela and I at the time.. One day, shortly after purchasing our new home, I arrived home early from work. When I pulled into our garage, I noticed a school bus in the driveway and Samantha getting off the bus. I knew that she did not live in the school district and was puzzled as to how this came to be. So, I asked him about this.

"Oh, *we* decided that *we* wanted her to go to school in a better school district, so *we* are using our address," Love responded in a defensive tone as if I had no business asking about this.

"We?" I responded with a hint of black girl attitude. The word that echoed in my head was *we* which didn't include me as his wife but included a home where I lived and paid half the bills. I was bothered by this. I was bothered not for the reason that Love had convinced himself. I was bothered by the simple fact that Love had made a decision about the use of our marital home with his ex-wife and had failed to inform me, his current wife. I tried to stay rational and used this as an opportunity to discuss my feelings.

"So, when were you going to inform me about yall's decision?" I asked, referring to Love and his ex-wife.

Like clock-work, this turned into an argument. Instead of Love seeing that I was upset about his lack of consideration for me as his wife, I was immediately accused of the extreme of not wanting his daughter to go to a good school. I was frustrated with his takeaway from the dialogue but this was not uncommon. It was easier for him to make me the villain in our conversations by accusing me of not wanting Samantha to go to a good school than for him to take accountability for the fact that his failure to inform me was a problem.

"Did you ask *my* permission for Madison to use this address to go to the school here?" He retorted angrily.

I stood there confused trying to figure out whether this was a trick question. Madison lived in the home which was in the district where she would be going to school which he was aware of. How did we start using permission and informed as synonyms? Discussion with Love often felt like going in circles with a five-year-old, so I didn't even bother to respond to this statement to avoid the circular conversation that was sure to come. After several attempts at a rational conversation, I decided to keep my thoughts to myself.

Love's response and other accusatory responses of this nature made me question his priorities as well as my role in this now blended family. I was uncomfortable with him making decisions with his ex-wife about our home which excluded me. I wasn't demanding permission. I just wanted to be informed. Additionally, I wondered why my entire character had to rest on this request.

Similar instances of this nature would occur leaving me clueless about what was going on in my own home. Questions about these incidents and attempts to have healthy discussions would quickly escalate into heated arguments ending with me being the villain. It was as though he felt he didn't need to talk to me about issues related to Samantha. He absolutely did not owe me any explanation when it came to how he and Pamala decided to parent. However, when those parenting decisions involved a home that we shared, I expected to be notified. Over time, he had simply convinced himself that I simply didn't like Samantha. It was easier for him to think this way and relieved him of any responsibility to make changes.

"You don't care for my child," he would frequently accuse.

Every weekend visit became an opportunity for Love to search, scrutinize, and store up examples of something I did or didn't do to support this ridiculous belief. He carried this belief throughout the entire marriage periodically bringing up something I did or failed to do as a stepmother during unrelated arguments. Normal relationship misses and misunderstanding would result in automatic charges. I never knew what charge I was going to be hit with when it came to his Samantha. I always felt like I was under his watchful eye to see if I talked sixty seconds longer to Madison than I did to Samantha, or if I put more macaroni on Madison's plate than Samantha. Visitation weekends eventually became very uncomfortable and dreadful. It became a tense environment where everything seemed forced and transactional. Just like it was easier for Love to believe that I didn't like Samantha, it honestly became much easier for me to avoid contact, just stay out of the way and stay off his radar.

As a therapist, I am aware of the struggles that come along with blending families from previous relationships. But arguing about one child all the time was disturbing for me. With all the other issues in the marriage, this appeared to be his one and only concern. As time went on, there was indeed a breakdown in the progression of our family blending. While interactions were reduced to normal pleasantries and greetings of *hello, goodbye, see you later,* there was no deliberate mistreatment of any kind as Love would like to insinuate.

I once bought Samantha a gift card for her birthday. Since she was not over during the week, I gave the gift card to Love to give to her on my behalf since he frequently saw her during the week between bi-weekly visitations. I noticed that he had left the gift card sitting on our bedroom dresser for several days. Attempting to stay in the lane he made clear was mine, I tried not to mention anything about it. A few days after Samantha finally did come over for her weekend visitation the card remained on the dresser. Unable to hold my peace any longer, I inquired. His response reiterated the watchful eye that I had unknowingly been under the entire time and would now be charged for.

"I was just gonna let it sit here and wait to see if you were going to offer to give it to her. We don't want it anymore. You can give it to Madison," Love replied angrily.

Giving Samantha the gift card was not the issue for me. What bothered me was the manipulative intent behind his delay in giving her the gift card that I voluntarily purchased. I was being tested and had failed. Additionally, I was held responsible for her not receiving the card in a timely manner.

"You can go ahead and give it to Madison. We don't want it now," he reiterated nonchalantly. This casual, cavalier attitude angered me, but this was not an uncommon response from him in the blended family process.

Love also had a teenage daughter, Jade, from a different relationship. I found the relationship between him and Jade to be a bit strained and disconnected. I always advocated for his relationship with Jade and encouraged him to be just as present and intentional with her as he was with Samantha. If I'm honest, a part of me recalled being in Jade's position; holding the title as the first-born daughter, but not having the benefit of a solid relationship with your dad like he had with his other children. I was there for pictures with Jade on prom night, chipped in for her prom dress and attended her graduation dinner. My intentions were good. I had hoped to develop a stronger relationship with Jade while also bringing her and Love together. Unfortunately, this did not come to reality.

When Jade graduated from high school, I reached out to her to arrange to send her some graduation money. I sent a text asking if there was anything specific that she needed before leaving for school.

"I'm good. I'm already gone," she texted back.

Not thinking much of the brief response, I responded by offering to send cash instead and asked for her mailing address. To my surprise, this text conversation escalated to her mother and the next incoming text messages were full paragraph-style text messages from her. To my surprise, I was being accused of stealing Jade's college money of which I was totally clueless. Her mother further told me that I was overstepping my boundaries with Jade. She instructed me to never contact Jade again to which I apologetically agreed. What I found more disturbing was that all these accusations and character assaults were communicated in a group text between Jade and her mother who laughed and used scripture to taunt and support my impending spiritual consequences as a thief.. This eventually turned into a catty war of words as I clapped back. I felt disrespected, confused, and justified in defending myself.

Under the erroneous assumption that Love was going to come to my defense as my husband and clear things up, I forwarded all the nasty text messages to him and confidently waited until he got home.

"Wait till my husband sees this," I proudly told a co-worker who was aware of the brewing drama.

The response I received from him shocked and angered me and again left me questioning my place in the blended family hierarchy.

"I'm trying to build a relationship with my daughter and you are interfering with that. You should have just left it alone when she said that she did not need anything from you instead of trying to make her take money from you," he exclaimed angrily when he walked in the house that day.

To my disappointment, I was being corrected instead of being protected. I wondered if he had actually read the disrespectful text messages that were sent to me that day and the accusations that I stole money from her. I wondered if he could see that I was just trying to help. Confused and angry, I tried to defend myself and argue my position. But Love made it clear that I was not the priority. Another round of the silent treatment started and like clockwork he eventually left the house. Devastated and hurt, I sat down on the bathroom floor as I frequently did when distressed. I found the tile floor to be a cool, dry area that soothed me. "How could he not support me or even hear me?" I thought as the tile floor caught my tears.

Love walked back into the room where I sat on the floor crying. He said not a word as he walked right past me. I was being punished with a familiar silence. He took a shower, dressed, and left the house again without saying a word. My lashes filled with tears and dripped to the tile floor. I tried to figure out what I did wrong. I considered the possibility that everything was indeed my fault.

Later that day, I wrote Love an apology letter apologizing for interfering in his relationship with Jade. I knew that my intentions were good, but I was not yet familiar with gaslighting and other abuse tactics that came along with toxic relationships. I had allowed Love to gaslight me into believing I had done something wrong and owed him an apology.

I placed the three-page handwritten letter on our bedroom dresser right where he had previously left the gift card I had purchased for Samantha. The silent treatment continued into the night so I slept in the guest room hoping that space would give him time to read my letter. The next afternoon I inquired.

"Did you get the letter I wrote to you? I asked timidly.

"I saw it, but I didn't read it," Love replied with a familiar casual and cavalier tone.

Hurt, I took the letter back and filed it away. The wounding message that my words and feelings didn't matter pierced my spirit. Once we did talk about it, it was clear that he still blamed me for interfering in his relationship with Jade. I had once again gotten out of my lane. Love listed all the things I should and should not have done in that situation with Jade. I felt like a scolded child and was left with the lingering question, was that my fault? But I also had the brewing question of, where was my place in this marriage? I had always believed in the traditional order of things, God, spouse, and children. Love's responses were causing me to question his values in this area. To me, we were totally out of order.

The totality of his responses to me when it came to his children further impacted my participation in the blending efforts not because I did not care for his children, as he became committed to believing, but because I felt stuck in trying to figure out my role and where I fit. If I was proactive and got too involved, I was charged with interference and overstepping my boundaries. If I was reserved and stayed in my lane, I was charged with not doing enough. There were no clear boundaries established in the marriage. I felt out of place and out of order.

A part of me also felt insecure. I never really knew how to comfortably *be* with either of his children as I questioned my role in their lives and my place in his. I felt confused. We needed to talk about it...I needed to talk about it. I tried to explain these things to Love in another failed attempt to talk things out like two adults and come to a healthy resolution. But again, Love was not skilled at healthy communication.

"Man, What?! That's bullshit. I'm not buying that! You can save that," Love responded as he dismissed my attempts to explain my struggles in the area.

These unresolved boundary issues made an already difficult situation even more difficult.

During discussions about ways to reconcile his relationship with Jade, he confidently told me that he believed with time, things would eventually improve on their own without any effort from him. I adopted that same magical thinking as it related to my relationship with her. I was not afforded use of this same mindset. In his mind, I needed to take action. It never felt like there was any real room for the relationships to evolve freely. Everything felt transactional and scrutinized.

While arguments always seemed to revolve around some supposed failure surrounding *his* children on my part, no one seemed to talk about the fact that Madison seemed detached and indifferent. The one time I did bring something to Love's attention pertaining to her expressed concerns about his kicking me, it turned into an argument. Madison was now on trial and being accused of being the problem child in the marriage as a result of her expressing concerns and not just quietly going with the status quo.. That would be the last time I would come to him about concerns expressed by Madison. She had fallen into what is commonly known in a narcissistic family system as the scapegoat child. I knew it wasn't emotionally safe for her either.

Attempts to have hard conversations with Love about blended issues proved ineffective so I eventually stopped trying. Looking back, I recognize that his commitment to the story in his head about me not liking his children served him in a way. It gave him a reason to devalue me and my character to himself and other people. Sadly, some of them believed him. Looking back, I wish I had gotten out of my head and taken a bigger stance when addressing this issue. I accept that while I did not do anything to hurt the situation, I did not do much to help improve the situation either.

The good news is that although the blended family problems were unable to be resolved through conversation while being married to Love, my eventual relationship with Pamela provided an opportunity to restore and heal any unintended damage that was caused to either of our girls as a result of the adults in their lives being unable to get it together. After years of believing that Pamela was mean and unreasonable, I found her to be sweet, funny, and supportive when it came to the blending of our families. I even learned that Pamela had my name listed as Samantha's emergency contact at the school and that she was under the impression that Love and I had discussed their school district decision. Pamela and I were able to talk like adults. We put aside our differences only to discover that we were not so different after all. Our relationship and ability to work together set the tone for restructuring the relationship with our girls.

Love was too committed to the belief that I didn't like Samantha to see that my daughter had needs too. He also missed the fact that both girls required much more than gifts and trips out of town and that they were both smarter than the adults in their lives had given them credit. Pamela and I celebrated the restructuring of the relationships by renting a condo and taking Madison and Samantha on a girl's trip to the beach. Pamela and Samantha have even come by the house to visit on occasions. A beautiful thing happens when healthy minded people work together. My relationship with Jade remains unresolved but I wish her well.

Chapter 10
Narcissistic Personality Disorder and Narcissistic Abuse

The people perish from lack of knowledge
Hosea 4:6

T his chapter may get a little clinical. But I ask that you stay with me as it will be helpful in determining whether you are in a relationship with someone with narcissistic traits or someone who is simply toxic which I am convinced that I was. The terms narcissist, narcissism, or Narcissistic Personality Disorder (NPD) seem to be thrown around casually in this day and age. Everyone seems to be narcissistic and everyone seems to be an expert offering their own counsel and advice on the subject. From movies to TV to social media, everyone seems to be operating with a Google license to label someone as a narcissist. As a licensed mental health professional, I recognize the seriousness in slapping such a label on someone. I am also very careful about giving such a label or diagnosis even with an active license to do so. Narcissism is often referred to by clinicians as the diagnosis of inevitable harm. This is because you cannot stay in a relationship with someone with high narcissistic traits long term and not be harmed in some way.

Most therapists don't know how to help those impacted by this type of abuse because it often flies under the radar of treatment. Without missing teeth or black eyes, narcissistic abuse is often not recognized as abuse. I spent years in school being trained under the umbrella of the counseling, mental health, and the psychology profession. During my undergraduate and graduate school training, personality disorders were a topic that, looking back, I don't think received adequate attention. During my training, most of the mental health conditions that were the focus of clinical attention and still are today revolve around conditions such as Depression, Bipolar Disorder, Anxiety, Schizophrenia and Co-Occurring Disorders.

While these conditions are certainly important and worth attention, no one told us, or at least me, about the serious impact of emotional and psychological abuse that could occur at the hands of someone with high narcissist personality traits or Narcissistic Personality Disorder (NPD). Even with growing focus and acceptance on mental health treatment, many clinicians are not adequately trained to recognize the unique needs of victims of this type of insidious abuse or to effectively help them. In a couple's session, for instance, some therapists have even been known to take the side of the abuser leaving the victim feeling further alone.

This form of abuse is so hidden that it's often hard for others to believe you without physical proof. I have been on both sides of the coin. Not only am I a therapist licensed to treat and diagnose, I am also a survivor. This, I believe, puts me in a unique position to speak on the topic.

While not all inclusive, it is my intention during this chapter to provide you with information that was not provided to me during my graduate training regarding NPD. I will provide you with not only a clinical explanation of NPD and the phases of NPD abuse; I will also provide you with information on common terms and behaviors for recognizing and describing experiences common to those involved in relationships with narcissists or those with high narcissistic traits. Later, I will use my own personal story and interactions with Love as a guide to help you identify the stages and red flags of abuse in your own relationship.

Finally, this information is in no way intended for you to go around labeling people as narcissistic. Only a trained professional can diagnose someone as having NPD. Instead, it is my hope that you come to recognize the pattern of crazy-making behaviors that come with these types of toxic relationships in order to protect yourself before too much emotional and psychological damage is done. I also encourage you to research these terms on your own to become more familiar with them. You will have to determine for yourself whether coping within the relationship is costing you too much.

What is a personality Disorder?

Before we get into NPD and the phases of narcissistic abuse, let me give you a very brief overview about what a personality disorder is. A personality disorder is classified as a mental health condition. Clinically, these mental health conditions fall into a category of their own and should not be confused with organic mental health conditions such as Depression, Bipolar Disorder, Anxiety, Schizophrenia and other co-Occurring Disorders. However, many people with personality disorders do suffer from some of these conditions as well and likely have some history of trauma.

Narcissistic personality disorder (NPD), is one of nine personality disorders. According to the Diagnostic and Statistical Manual of Mental Disorders 5th edition, NPD is characterized by someone who has a persistent manner of grandiosity, a continuous desire for admiration, along with a lack of empathy. It starts by early adulthood and occurs in a range of situations, as signified by the existence of any 5 of the next 9 standards (American Psychiatric Association, 2015):

- A grandiose logic of self-importance

- A fixation with fantasies of infinite success, control, brilliance, beauty, or idyllic love

- A credence that he or she is extraordinary and exceptional and can only be understood by, or should connect with, other extraordinary or important people or institutions

- A desire for unwarranted admiration

- A sense of entitlement

- Interpersonally oppressive behavior

- No form of empathy

- Resentment of others or a conviction that others are resentful of him or her

- A display of egotistical and conceited behaviors or attitudes

The description given above is helpful when providing a diagnosis to insurance companies or informing clinical practice for treating someone in a clinical setting. What this description does not do is give a breakdown of terminology and behavioral examples that may prepare and protect others from the emotional and psychological damage that comes along from being involved with individuals with these traits. It is very possible to have high NPD traits and not have the diagnosis. Regardless, toxic behaviors are enough to cause damage.

Covert vs. Overt Narcissist

While the DSM-5's description of NPD suggests a single type of narcissist, more research is recognizing the existence of subtypes of this disorder. The two I want to focus on are the covert and the overt types.

Our classic overt type (observable) is the typical arrogant and self-absorbed type. These individuals may appear loud and self-centered and may exploit others for their own personal gain. The covert type, on the other hand, is, in my humble opinion, more dangerous and harmful because their abuse is more subtle. Coverts, meaning hidden, are quiet, shy, and may even come off as insecure. Their covert abusive ways are so hidden and sneaky that many people on the outside would find it difficult to believe that they would behave in abusive ways. This is the quiet girl or guy at the party who doesn't talk much in public, but will find out all your insecurities and use them as weapons against you to win an argument behind closed doors.

While narcissism falls on a spectrum from high to low, what most narcissists share, whether covert or overt, is a **lack of genuine empathy.** I say genuine because any empathy that they do show is a mask or done with some personal gain in mind. Cognitive empathy is often used by these personalities. This type of empathy does not require any emotional connection or compassion. In romantic relationships, it is not uncommon for narcissists to watch their intended targets long enough, via social media for example, to determine their likes and to act on them. This is called mirroring. They might become experts at mirroring the desires and emotions of their intended targets so they can pretend to share their interests and then hook them in.

The problem with mirroring is that over time the narcissist can't keep up the charade. Their mask will eventually begin to slip and their true self will be exposed. By and by, they will grow tired of pretending and suddenly the very things that they like about you become irritants. It's the classic bait and switch except now you are all in and desperately trying to get back the person you thought you knew.

Love bombing is a tactic used by highly narcissistic personalities whereby they shower you with love, affection, attention, and gifts. This is usually done very early in the relationship. While the love bombing feels good to us, it is also the very thing that gets us hooked. This is why we experience such discomfort when they suddenly pump the brakes or withdraw their love and affection. What's important to remember here is that everything is conditional…even the love bombing.

Blame shifting is a common tactic used when you are in relationship with a person with toxic or high narcissistic traits. If you confront them with something they did to hurt you that day, they will tell you about something you did to hurt them last year and place the entire blame for the current and past issue on you. Trying to resolve conflict with a narcissist will leave you exhausted and confused. You will find that you are never quite able to get to the current issue due to talking about unresolved issues from the past. This involves what's called circular conversation and word salad.

The silent treatment and withdrawing love and affection occur often as a form of punishment when you "misbehave" in these toxic relationships. It should be noted, normal relationships require a break sometimes. The difference is that this is communicated and both parties can agree to discuss the issue later. On the contrary, not with a narcissist. They will deflect, avoid, and never take any accountability for their role in the breakdown. In addition to punishment, the silent treatment reflects their emotional immaturity and inability to have healthy conversations.

Object Consistency is another important term to know when dealing with someone with high narcissistic traits. This term speaks to the black or white, good or bad thinking of a narcissist in relationships. Healthy-minded people have the ability to see people they are involved with as lovable and valuable even if they are imperfect or do something "wrong." Conversely, a narcissist cannot see you this way. They struggle to see others as fallible and lovable at the same time. Again, with a narcissist, you are either all good or all bad..no in-between. Your entire character will often be judged by your current mistake. Additionally, narcissists struggle with genuine attachment to people because they never really connect with anyone in the first place which makes it easy for them to simply disconnect and discard. They can shift from loving you to hating you very quickly because the love was most likely never genuine.

Many narcissists are extremely concerned with their image and the way people see them. In fact, they are generally more concerned with the way the public sees them for their toxic behaviors than the way the victims they hurt see them. With this in mind, once you start speaking out against them, they may start with what's called a **smear campaign** against you. They may even accuse you of trying to start a smear campaign against them and accuse you of doing the things they themself are doing.

Keep in mind that there is a major difference between a smear campaign and speaking out. It all revolves around intention and motivation. A smear campaign is a collection of *lies* that never happened and are intended to harm a person's reputation or to get some external gain. Speaking out is a way to tell your story, reclaim your voice, and help educate others along the way.

Bread crumbing is another common term used throughout the NPD abuse community and goes along with trauma bonding which I will discuss in detail in chapter twelve. During the love bombing phase, high levels of dopamine are received making you feel good. When the toxic person withdraws love and affection as punishment for some perceived slight, those levels drop leaving you feeling bad. At this point, you just want to make up and get back to normal again. Bare minimum acts of kindness known as bread crumbing, suddenly become enough to keep you on your best behavior with the narcissist, hoping at some point to get back to the love bombing. The act of breadcrumbing is equivalent to starving a person of food and then giving them bread crumbs to make them feel better, thus the term breadcrumbing.

Gaslighting is a strategy used to make the target doubt their reality. It sends you down the road of crazy-making conversation and may cause you to doubt yourself. Telling half-truths or making up things that never happened is a form of gaslighting. If you express your feelings or become emotional and are made to feel that your feelings and emotions are the problem instead of their behavior that contributed to them, you have experienced gaslighting. Another example is being made to believe that there is not a problem in the relationship, despite your observations of being treated with silence. You are left to figure out what the problem is on your own or settle with the false reality that you are just too sensitive or overreacting. Meanwhile, there was some perceived slight that occurred, unbeknownst to you, that is now being held in the fault valut for a later argument. The goal of gaslighting is to leave you confused and rattled with self-doubt.

Projection occurs when the narcissist accuses you of being the narcissist. They simply dump their nasty traits onto you, making you the villain in the story. Considering that self-reflection and accountability is like kryptonite to someone with high narcissistic traits, this also allows them to maintain their good guy or good girl role also known as their *false self*. During periods of projections, their accusations that you are the one behaving badly, may leave you questioning yourself. They may even go so far as to try to convince others, including your friends and family, that *you* are a narcissist. What's worse is that they are often successful in convincing people of this.

Connected with this is **triangulation**. This is when a third party is pulled into the relationship conflict and used against you. If you were adopted or have a poor relationship with your family, for example, they may triangulate by bringing this up in an argument and saying something like "That is why your own mother/family doesn't like you." Lies and twisted narratives about you are often spoken to others behind your back in an effort to get others to side with them. Sadly, many times they do. This is where the flying monkeys come on the scene. The flying monkeys are the friends and family members who blindly support the abuser. They believe their lies, do their bidding, and abuse you by proxy.

Reactive abuse is a term used to describe the reaction of a victim in response to being constantly provoked by a toxic person and then accused of being the abusive person. For example, during a verbal argument with your partner, he or she physically restrains you to prevent you from walking away from them. When verbal instructions for them to let you go fail, you physically snatch your body away from them causing them to fall backward and hit their head on the floor. You are then accused of being the abuser. They can't see their contribution of their initial behavior to the outcome, only how your behavior caused them to get injured.

A red flag of a narcissistic relationship is the time frame with which these relationships progress. Romantic relationships with a narcissist move quickly. One minute you are getting to know each other, the next minute you are talking about moving in together and getting married. People with high narcissistic traits typically move from one romantic relationship to another and may get re-married very quickly after being divorced.

The cycle in a toxic or narcissistic relationship typically unfolds in a very clear pattern of idealization and love bombing, devaluation, and discard which I will discuss in detail in the next chapter. The cycle often repeats itself and if not recognized, can slowly chip away at who you are. To help you recognize this pattern, I will demonstrate what this looks like using my personal experiences with Love from the beginning of our courtship and marriage and into the dissolution of it in the next chapter.

Chapter 11
The Cycle of Violence and Narcissistic Abuse

People will be lovers of themselves, lovers of money, boastful, proud, abusive, disobedient to their parents, ungrateful, unholy, without love, unforgiving, slanderous, without self-control, brutal, not lovers of the good, treacherous, rash, conceited, lovers of pleasure rather than lovers of God— having a form of godliness but denying its power. Have nothing to do with such people. They are the kind who worm their way into homes and gain control over gullible women, who are loaded down with sins and are swayed by all kinds of evil desires, always learning but never able to come to a knowledge of the truth.
2 Timothy 3: 2-7

When we talk about abuse today, we tend to automatically think of it only within the context of physical abuse. However, all abuse is not physical. As mentioned in previous chapters, one of the worst kinds of abuse is non-physical injuries that result from emotional and psychological abuse. Further complicating things is the fact that society has yet to fully acknowledge abuse unless it is accompanied by black eyes and broken bones. Psychological abuse can be so hidden that survivors may find themselves questioning whether it was actually abuse. The lack of physical evidence often sends people into hiding and the abuser flies under the radar.

I spent five years in a marriage with a man who was emotionally and on occasion, physically abusive. Toward the end of the marriage he was also sexually exploitive. As discussed in previous chapters, the problem for many people in these types of relationships is that the person is not abusive every day. There are happy times between each cycle of abuse which resets a false hope that things will improve. This may even create self-doubt about whether the experience was actually abuse.

The purpose of this next section is to help you examine your relationship by identifying the cycle of violence and phases of narcissistic abuse for yourself. It is my hope that this information will further help eliminate any self-doubt you may be experiencing in your present relationship or resolve those in the past that have come to an end . The cycle of abuse, also known as the cycle of violence, includes four distinct phases represented by the following stages:

Tensions build

Abusive partners often lash out in response to external stressors. Anything can fuel tension: family issues, trouble at work, physical illness, fatigue.

Frustration and dissatisfaction intensify over time, often prompting feelings of powerlessness, injustice, anger, and paranoia.

Sensing the simmering tension, you might try to find ways to placate the abusive partner and prevent abuse from happening.

You may feel anxious, on your guard, and hyper alert to their potential needs. You might alternate between tiptoeing around them, trying not to set them off, and making an extra effort to provide physical and emotional support.

Incident of abuse or violence

The abuser eventually releases this tension on others, attempting to regain power by establishing control.

Abuse might involve:

- Insults or name-calling
- Using your past or present vulnerabilities as a way to hurt you
- Threats of harm or property destruction
- Attempts to control your behavior
- Threats to abandon you

- Sexual or physical violence
- Emotional manipulation
- They might accuse you of making them mad or blame you for your "relationship problems."

Keep in mind that people choose to abuse others. Any tension they experience may help explain the abuse, but it never excuses it.

Reconciliation

After the incident of abuse, tension gradually begins to fade. In an attempt to move past the abuse, the abuser often uses kindness, gifts, and loving gestures to usher in a "honeymoon" stage.

This devoted behavior can trigger the release of dopamine and oxytocin, helping you feel even more closely bonded and leading you to believe you have your "real" relationship back.

Calm Again

To maintain peace and harmony, both parties generally have to come up with some sort of explanation or justification for the abuse.

The abusive partner might:

- Apologize while blaming others
- Point to outside factors to justify their behavior
- Minimize the abuse or deny it happened
- Accuse you of provoking them

They might show plenty of remorse, assure you it won't happen again, and seem more attuned to your needs than usual. You might begin to accept their excuses and doubt your own memory of the abuse thinking, maybe it really was nothing like they said.

This reprieve offers relief from the physical and emotional tension and pain.

You might feel certain that whatever upset them and triggered the abuse has passed. You can't believe they'd do anything like that again.

Rinse and repeat

This cycle then repeats over time.

This "cycle" happens over and over within abusive relationships though. The length of time between each repetition can vary. It often is shortened over time as the abuse escalates.

As time goes on, the calm period may become very short or even disappear from the cycle entirely.

The cycle of narcissistic abuse has a distinct process that is often intertwined within the cycle of violence. This includes idealization and love bombing, devaluation and then discard. Reflecting back, I can clearly see the cycle and phases as they played out in my marriage. Unfortunately, I couldn't see it until it was too late. Sometimes you have to get away from the problem to recognize just how bad it is.

As you read my story, you may discover that you too missed or ignored similar red flags in your own relationships. Don't feel bad and don't beat yourself up. I spent years in school obtaining all types of fancy counseling degrees in the field. I still missed it and ended up married to a person who I am convinced was a covert narcissist. The other thing to remember is that people with high narcissistic traits typically show up as different people in the beginning of the relationship than who they reveal themselves to be in the end. Had we seen who they really were in the beginning, we would have never given them the time of day. So, don't be too hard on yourself.

Additionally, prepare yourself for the fact that there are going to be people who will not believe you. There were and will always be people who will struggle to believe that there exists a cold, vindictive abusive side of the person you experienced behind closed doors. They will cling to the positive image of those people in their minds. As humans, it is easier for us to discredit someone's claim of abuse than it is to reconcile in our minds that the person we knew to be kind could be the total opposite. Don't let that be your focus. Sharing your story could be someone else's survival guide.

Remember, a person with narcissistic character traits, particularly the covert kind, has spent his or her entire life convincing people that they are *the good guy or good girl* who always finishes last. This victim mask hides their true identity from family and friends who may have never seen that abusive side of them. It may be difficult for others to believe that the kind person they knew publicly was a monster to you privately. There is a community of survivors who can testify to the devastation and inevitable harm that relationships with toxic people can have. There is also clear and consistent research on the pattern of idealization, devaluation, and discard that show up while in relationship with toxic people. Identifying someone as a narcissist is not as important as recognizing the patterns and getting out safely.

The following is my story. Every one of these events is true. They were all documented in detail in my journal entries from over the past five years which I used in addition to therapy to cope. My goal is to bring awareness to signs and patterns so that we as a society can stop normalizing this level of dysfunction in relationships. I also want people to recognize that no one is 100% immune from finding themselves in these types of relationships.. not even mental health professionals.

Idealization and "Love Bombing" Phase

Falling in Love with Love

December 4, 11:35 am (Facebook Mailbox)
Love: I know you don't check your inbox so you might not see this message. There is nothing more attractive and intriguing than a woman that is smart, beautiful, and successful and on top of that, a good mother. I have been checking you out and I am not a stalker.

December 5, 1:05pm (Facebook Mailbox)
Me: LOL. Good afternoon. Thank you so much, I appreciate that. I am just checking my inbox. You are right. I hardly ever check it. LOL.

Love: I understand. I would love to meet you for lunch.

December 8, 12:04 (Facebook Mailbox)
Love: I admire your strength and your faith

December 9, 2:58 pm (Facebook Mailbox)

Me: Thank you so much. It's all God. He is the MAN! LOL.

Love: Here is my phone number. If possible, I want to take you to lunch

Me: I'm not sure: I really don't do hookups on social media

Love: I understand. That's why I recommended lunch. You can choose the time and the place and if you don't want to go out again, I promise I won't bother you again

Me: Ok. I have the number. Let me think on this.

Love: Ok. ☺

December 15, 7:41PM (Facebook Mailbox)

Love: I'm still waiting. "In my Jodeci Voice" LOL

Me: LOL

Love: How about a cup of coffee?

Me: Sure

Love: When?

Somewhere during this exchange, Love and I went to lunch at a local Japanese restaurant. Honestly, there was not an immediate attraction to or interest in him. It was his consistency that won me over and looking at his social media profile, he seemed like a sweet guy, quiet even. He was different from anyone I ever went out with before.

I remembered his shy, soft-spoken manner as he looked down at his chicken and shrimp hibachi on our first date. He didn't talk much, which was a concern for me, but I did my best to keep the conversation going. I shared with him that I was briefly married before but was now divorced.

"Yeah, I'm going through a divorce right now," he says, never looking up from his food.

"Wait. Hold on. So, you are married?" I asked in surprise.

106

"Yes. But it's been over. We go to court in June and the divorce will be final then."

"But you guys still live together?" I inquired looking at him.

"Yeah, but we sleep in separate rooms for like the last few years."

He went on to share with me how horrible of a person and mother she was; how she left her room and closets dirty and that he even had pictures in his phone to prove it. He told me that he eventually got tired of her not wanting to work and decided to divorce her. He added that she had held up the divorce process for several years. Something about it all still sounded suspect. Additionally, I knew how that whole married man business worked and I just wasn't interested.

I shared with Love that I thought it was best that we did not see each other anymore. Disappointed, he expressed understanding but assured me that he was *coming back* for me as soon as his divorce was final.

"I'm going to come back for you," he promised. I didn't count on it; however, a part of me wondered what it would be like for a man to keep such a promise to me. I didn't hold my breath.

Months passed and while we never went out again, Love would still like all my pictures on social media. He would shoot me a text every now and then to make sure I was still single. I sent him a congratulatory text when he announced via social media that he had graduated from his Master's degree program. There were brief phone conversations, most of which consisted of updating me on the divorce process and telling me how bad his ex-wife was and how she didn't feed their daughter.

March 4 2015 7:34 am (Facebook Mailbox)

Love: Did you change your number?

Me: No, I didn't. Why?

Love: I texted you last night

Me: Oh. I got it. I was half asleep. Went to bed early. I meant to reply but when I opened my eyes again, it was time for work. Missed my show and everything

Love: Oh. Ok. I miss talking to you.

On June 1, before the ink was dry in his divorce decree, Love reached out to me via text telling me that he had gone to court that day and that he was officially divorced. Our world wind romance began with Love inviting me on a weekend trip to Dallas at the end of June. I initially had concerns about the sleeping arrangements. My concerns were put to rest when Love agreed to my request for separate beds. I was swept off my feet! Not only had this man kept his promise to *come back* for me, he also agreed to get two beds for the hotel. He was so kind to me and was a perfect gentleman the entire time. His sweet and gentle demeanor made me feel safe. I excitedly told my friends about this.

The Dallas trip was followed by more trips as well as gifts in the form of jewelry and flowers. He would text me lengthy love songs which made me blush. He knew I loved sweets, so he would always bring me a slice of his mother's famous pound cake. One day he came to my job to surprise me with a pair of gold Michael Kors earrings. While I was not a woman who required *things*, his token of kindness felt really nice. As I leaned in to thank him with a hug that day, he whispered ever so gently in my ear.

"You are going to be my wife."

We had only been dating two months. But the excitement of his words put me on cloud nine!

Things moved quickly. We traveled together and spent time enjoying each other's company. Love spent a lot of time at my house. He even agreed to sleep in my guest room in the beginning of our relationship out of my concern for Madison seeing a man there. After all, it had been just she and I for some time.

Unfortunately, residual drama from his recent divorce was just getting started. Although the divorce was final, so I thought, the division of assets was not complete. This left the issue of the marital property where his ex-wife and daughter continued to live unresolved. I tried my best to stay out of that. I was so caught up in the dopamine of his kindness that I blindly believed what he told me about his ex-wife and their legal woes. I allowed him to convince me that she was the problem.

One day Love took my daughter and his daughter, Samantha, to the house where his ex-wife and child still lived to pick up some clothes. We were talking on the phone when suddenly a heated argument ensued between him and his ex-wife. All I could hear was him yelling and her in the background yelling back. I had never heard him yell like that before. It was scary. I called his name but could not get his attention. It was like he was in an angry demonic trance. Suddenly the call was disconnected. I tried to call him back but didn't get an answer. My mind immediately switched to Madison. He had my child with him and I panicked at the thought of her being around the level of chaos I was hearing.

When I finally got him on the phone he was frustrated, loud and stuttered through his words. He told me about a plant that belonged to his deceased cousin that apparently his ex-wife had sold. Apparently, this was the cause of the heated argument I had borne witness to. I listened as he reiterated all the negative character traits he had previously told me about his ex-wife and how she deliberately sold his plant. While I tried to be empathetic, there was a part of me that was disturbed by the fact that a grown man would respond that way over a plant.

Madison later told me that Samantha had run into the closet during the argument and covered her ears... a response that disturbed me. I had a conversation with Love about my position on arguing in front of my daughter and kids in general. Madison's dad and I had only done that once and I vowed never to do that again. Love appeared receptive and assured me it wouldn't happen again. I looked over the incident and went back to my cloud number nine.

Our relationship continued to move quickly. Love started to attend church with me, something that had always been very important. I was happy to introduce him to my church family. Love even showed an interest in prayer, spiritual things, and my position about us not having sex before marriage, although we kept slipping up. The fact that he cared about it made me happy. His mirroring act made me feel like I won.

One October while sitting on the couch in a bathrobe watching Tyler Perry's, "The Have and the Have Nots," Love pretended to be picking up something off the floor. To my surprise, he dropped down to my lap and produced a little white box. He popped it open and asked me to marry him. This was done privately at home in front of the TV, nothing fancy, but it was perfect. I said yes! We had only been dating a few months and I couldn't wait to tell Madison when she woke up. Now, I could finally tell her that I was going to marry the man named "Love" I had always told her about.

I later discovered that while Love had indeed gone to court in June to finalize the divorce, it was not officially finalized until late August of that same year. We were engaged in October of that year. The timing made it appear that I had been in the picture all along. I was angry with Love who quickly smoothed things over by telling me his attorney told him that he was free to date after the June hearing after which he *came back for me*. The timing still felt off and I questioned whether it was too soon. Ignoring my internal alarms, I believed what he told me and went back to my cloud with my shiny little engagement ring.

The idealization continued with Love telling me how much different I was from his ex-wife, like he was marrying up. He was particularly bothered by the fact that his ex did not or would not work citing this as a deciding factor for divorcing her. He compared my work ethic and multiple streams of income with her supposed failure to do so. Intentionally or not, he sent the message that I was somehow *better* than her because of this. Ashamedly, I began to adopt such ignorant thinking. He even had me looking down on her for not working without knowing her full story.

We had a small wedding. The venue was well decorated. The limo was parked outside as we said our I do's in the presence of God, friends, and family. I felt so beautiful as a bride and filled with excitement. My big day had finally come.

After the wedding, Love officially joined my church and immediately jumped into service, mirroring my interests. I was already serving as a greeter when we met so he joined the usher department and became an active member of the church's Ministry of Defense. I felt like we were the ultimate power couple serving together. Over time, the displays of love through gifting became less frequent. Seeing as though I wasn't a person who required a lot of *things* to be happy, it didn't bother me much. The occasional surprise of my favorite cookie was enough to keep me satisfied.

What I truly desired from Love was never financial. What I wanted and needed was communication and connection, particularly during bad times. For me, being kind and emotionally connected during good times was easy. I was turned on by the challenge of being able to offer love and respect during bad times. That was an ongoing challenge for us that never seemed to resolve itself. Things between us slowly fell apart.

The Devaluation Phase

"I dreaded coming here with you. I was going to buy you a big rock for our anniversary, but I knew something like this was going to happen. If I had brought that teacher who I was messing around with all the way to Cancun, she would have dropped her panties for me in the middle of the floor as soon as we got here. But not you. You come here complaining." Love lashed out as he sat on the edge of the bed of our Cancun hotel room. We had been married five years and the love felt like it was gone.

My heart sank. A familiar ache stretched across my chest. I felt hopeless and embarrassed. Not only was my husband comparing me to another woman whom he had had a past sexual relationship with, he was also suggesting to me that I was not worth the ring he was supposedly going to buy me for our anniversary. I would have preferred that he just cancelled the trip before-hand if this was how he felt. I considered replying to his insults with a similar comparison of the men who had treated me better than he had; nevertheless, I decided against it. Not only could his fragile ego not take it, it would also be pointless to devalue him the way he was devaluing me. My goal was to reconcile with him, not to hurt him.

Cancun was not the first time I had experienced the devaluation phase with Love. As I reflect back on my journal entries, devaluation would happen frequently during heated arguments which would generally revolve around or be triggered by me expressing any emotions. In response, Love had conveniently convinced himself that my tears were simply not real.

About two months before our wedding day, Love and I took another trip out of town. On the way back there was an argument. For some reason arguments seemed to become more frequent on trips. He had convinced me that it was always *me* trying to start a fight. I began to wonder if it was true, if it was all me as he claimed.

We stopped at a local Applebee's in our home town before going home. We had a drink with an appetizer. Tensions escalated and we decided to leave the restaurant to make the 10-minute drive to my house. As we approached his truck, we continued to bicker. I still don't remember what the argument was about, but it became enough for me not to want to ride with him.

"I'm not getting in the truck. I will walk home," I said through my tears as I attempted to get whatever belongings I could gather out of his back seat.

After a few angry attempts to force me to get in the truck, I saw the crack in Love's mask for the second time. He said the words that I would have never thought I would hear him say to me.

"Well, fuck you then bitch," Love snapped.

The words rolled off his tongue with a sharp confident pierce. I was in shock but didn't stop walking. I listened as he started his truck and backed out of the parking space. He drove past me with aggression that could almost be felt. He turned the corner seemingly on two wheels and disappeared into the interstate traffic. I watched through falling tears as the truck we rode in together entered the on ramp and disappeared. Tears continued to spill out of my eyes and down my face as I looked down at my engagement ring through my tears. The wedding was less than two months away. Do I call it off? I couldn't think. I was too hurt. I began my on-foot commute home in tears. The 10-minute drive was now a 30-minute walk. As I entered the on-ramp, a female motorist pulled over. She and her adult daughter convinced me to allow them to take me home. I got in. I was desperate. I silently cried all the way home.

They dropped me off safely in front of my house. I walked up to the door only to discover that I had left my house keys in Love's truck. I reluctantly made the phone call to request my keys. His nonchalant tone angered and hurt me all at the same time.

"I'll be there in a little bit," he said before hanging up the phone.

I spent the next 15 minutes mentally replying to what had just happened. I cried and contemplated on what to do next. When he arrived, I walked to the truck to retrieve my keys and I turned to walk back to my house. He left without incident. Later that night he returned. He got down on his knees to apologize to me promising to never disrespect me that way again. The fact that he was sorry was all I needed. I was back on cloud nine.

As I reflect back over my journal entries after the wedding, I can recall a series of arguments that turned into nasty episodes of devaluation. I never understood how simple disagreements could get so bad so quickly or how Love could use some of my most vulnerable moments shared with him as ammunition.

"That's why Rejed didn't want you," he teased during another argument. "Had you sitting up crying and devastated over a nigga that didn't even want you. If it were not for me you would not even be married." I had mistakenly shared with him how devastated I was by the ending of my brief marriage to Rejed and there he was launching into an attack using it as ammunition to hurt me.

"Fuck you, Tiffany. You are a selfish mutha fucka. This is my damn TV and I can't even watch it when I want to," Love yelled as he stood from our bed and headed to the living room. This documented outburst was happening over the TV remote control and seemed to come out of nowhere. *How did my boundaries crumble to this?* I thought. I stayed silent, in total shock and disbelief, trying to figure out what in the world had just happened. I later came into the living room where Love was on the couch with a blanket.

"Here, Love. You can have the remote," I offered. "If it's all that serious you can have it."

Love refused. Like a five year old holding a grudge, he folded his arms and did not as much as look in my direction. This led to two days of the silent treatment and him sleeping in the spare guest room.

When I finally broke the ice and asked to discuss the issue, I was hit with charges that I didn't even realize I had. Love went from complaints about me hogging the remote at night, to me turning on the porch light while he was watching TV in the living room; to me leaving my shoes on the floor; to me having enough energy to go to the gym but not putting my shoes away; to his not being able to sleep in the mornings while I was getting ready for work because my heels were too loud across the floor. He was even talking about moving out and getting his own place. I was baffled. But as always, I was quick to forgive and found my way back to my cloud.

"Your entire family even knows that you have horrible character," he yelled from the bedroom as I spoke to my mother from a closet. Another round of devaluation was happening. Whatever the disagreement was this time, my entire character was now on the line and now, a recent disagreement with my family was being used to support his position. This demonstrated just how far he was willing to stoop to tear me down.

"You just wait until I turn that Facebook status to single and watch how many people get in my inbox," he once said to me. I didn't know whether to cry or laugh at his presumptuousness.

I would cry sometimes, but over time my tears stopped mattering to him. There was no empathy. There was no compassion. I eventually did my best to conceal my emotions around him. I knew it wasn't safe. To survive,

114

I created a safe space in the closet of one of my spare bedrooms where I learned to do all of my crying and praying. Sometimes I would cry so hard in there that I would cry myself to sleep right there in my prayer closet.

"You have two jobs, two houses, and two cars, and you are still unhappy. Who wouldn't be happy with all you have?" he yelled as he dismissed my tears and my need to connect on an emotional level. I felt totally unheard and dismissed. What I wanted from him meant so much more than material things.

When I told him I was going to take a drive to calm down, I suddenly became the bad guy because I was leaving.

"Narcissists always leave," he taunted. He then proceeded to pull out his cell phone, goggled narcissism, and began listing narcissistic traits. I recognized this as classic projection. I was still very disappointed.

This is exactly the kind of crazy making behaviors that go on in toxic relationships. Cycles of devaluation left me emotionally exhausted, broken and questioning if the horrible things he said were true. I knew Love would twist the truth and flat out lie to argue and support a weak point but I had hoped he would grow out of this toxic way of being.

To solve these heated arguments, we agreed to come up with a key word for either of us to use whenever things were getting heated and we needed to break. The goal was to communicate to the other that a break was needed from the argument, reset and to come back and talk again later. Once during a growing argument, I implemented the key word and asked for a 30-minute break. Love, however, insisted on talking right then. When I refused to engage in his forced efforts and set a boundary, he took off his wedding ring, threw it in my face and left the house.

"Only you know when enough is enough, Tiffany," I heard my mother's voice in my head again.

I used to be so strong and feisty. I suspect that I may have lost a little of that person over time in that marriage. Before I turned into an emotional mess with crumbing boundaries, there was a part of me who knew exactly who I was. I knew exactly how to roar and fight back with Love even if that meant going toe to toe with him in a verbal shouting match. But I never liked how I felt being that way. I wanted to love and be loved. I wanted to be protected and held. I wanted to make peace.

Once while on a weekend trip, Love and I had had a few too many drinks. Another argument ensued. I couldn't tell you what it was about if my life depended on it; nevertheless, I do remember that in response to Love's mocking and taunting, I told him that he was acting like an immature punk and that he needed to grow up. I will not try to justify or minimize my behavior. At the end of the day, it was disrespectful. I took full responsibility for my actions and apologized to Love.. Unfortunately, I would be sentenced and re-sentenced for that offense for years to come.

Instances like that from me, while wrong, were rare. Looking back, I wish I had stood up for myself more; consequently, I had a limit and knew what lines not to cross. I didn't want to get down in the mud and be nasty with Love the way he seemed to enjoy being with me. It was like it came normal for him. There was a level of nastiness and vindictiveness that came with his ways that I just couldn't get with. It was evil and sometimes frightened me.

The Discard Phase: The Grand Finale

The discard phase of a narcissistic or psychologically abusive relationship is very different from a normal, healthy relationship breakup. If you have ever been in a psychologically toxic or abusive relationship, you will find the discard phase is done in the nastiest way possible. It is deliberately evil and shaming, leaving you feeling like you have just been tossed from a moving relationship vehicle and like things were your fault. It often occurs suddenly, without warning, and may even happen on a special day such as your birthday or in my case, on the day of your wedding anniversary.

The interesting thing about the discard phase is that it can happen more than once. That was certainly the case for me during my marriage to Love. I cannot count how many times I was told he wanted a divorce throughout the course of our marriage. Divorce was always on the table. No pass go. No conversation. No compromise. Go straight to divorce. This pattern would leave me insecure after every disagreement frantically searching for evidence of our status.

I would search the drawers to see if he had removed his wedding ring, or, when the breadcrumbing began, look for whether or not he had left a bath towel out for me to determine if we were still good. I was often forced to look for divorce papers to determine our status after arguments when he would go silent. These are the things I had to do to determine our status and whether I had been discarded.

NO NORMAL RELATIONSHIP SHOULD PUT YOU IN A POSITION WHERE YOU ARE CONSTANTLY BEING THREATENED WITH ABANDONMENT OR QUESTIONING YOUR STATUS!
THAT IS NOT NORMAL. THAT IS A FORM OF ABUSE!

In addition to this, after each argument, I found myself self-reflecting on what I did wrong and what I should have done differently. I felt like a twelve-year old child who had misbehaved. If you were anything like me, you may have made frantic efforts to keep your relationship going, desperately wanting to get back to what you had in the beginning. Sadly, in psychologically toxic relationships, one of the hardest things to accept is the fact that those days were not real.

Over time, that push-and-pull way of being starts to deteriorate your self-worth. Arguments with Love left me filled with self-doubt and anxiety. As a therapist, I was well aware of my abandonment wounds. Unfortunately, so was Love as he would pick at these wounds during each disagreement.

"You are a fucking narcissist. I want a divorce," I remember him saying as I was discarded on our wedding anniversary in Cancun.

"You got your reaction out of me by trying to start an argument. He yelled as I cried. My desire to communicate my feelings was being equated to me trying to start a fight. While he remained interested in playing a game of *Guess the narcissist*, I ignored his projections and tried to focus on talking things out and reconciling. Ultimately, I just wanted to connect with him. *Maybe I was going about it wrong,* I doubted myself again

After our anniversary argument that day in Cancun, we talked things over and then went to dinner. Although it was still uncomfortable for me, acting like nothing happened and moving on was not uncommon. It soothed my anxiety, at least temporarily and left me with hope that once again, I could make us ok.

"I'll let my lady order first," he said, showing a glimpse of the man I fell in love with.

We had drinks, went dancing and returned to our hotel. Against my bodily desires, we made love that night. I cried silently the entire time. Eventually I felt the warm tears from my tears fall over the side of my face and roll into my ears. I kept thinking about the fact that I was giving my body to a man who three hours earlier was comparing me to another woman and telling me he wanted to divorce me. But I wanted to save our marriage. So, I was willing to bloom and sacrifice my body despite feeling emotionally raped in the process.

"Let's use a condom, please. We don't want any accidents right now," I whispered between heavy breaths as we kissed and touched.

"I'm not using a condom. You are *my* wife. You ain't going nowhere," Love said, breathing heavily into my ear as he reached his climax. I closed my eyes and let the sound of his voice fill my ear. I thought about his voice from five years earlier when he whispered into my ear that I was going to be his wife. I wanted that person back again. I pretended he was back. Despite what I knew, despite all that had happened, there in that moment, I still wanted my marriage. I still had hope that we could get back what we had. I didn't realize it then, but that night would be the last time we would ever make love.

Our last day in Cancun was quiet. We had breakfast on the balcony, drank mimosas, and chatted a bit. Things were getting back to what I had come to know as normal. The flight home was quiet and we even talked about how blessed we were to have the costumes and luggage processes go so smoothly. In my mind, we were going to be ok and start our five years together better. It wasn't until we got home and he slept on the couch that I realized that his status about our marriage had not changed

"I'm not happy. I don't want this marriage anymore. I told you in Cancun I wanted a divorce," Love said cold and matter-of-factly. I was discarded again.

I realized in that moment that his sleeping with me on that final night and refusing to use a condom was his sick and twisted way of hurting me in his grand finale. It worked. My last discard had to be the most painful. After unsuccessful negotiations and attempts to convince Love to fight for our marriage, I gave up. Shattered, I dropped the rope and released the marriage. But I certainly was not going to finance his decision.

Chapter 12
The Trauma Bond

Many victims of any form of abuse are often asked why they stayed. *If he or she was so abusive, then why did you stay?* This is a common but often unhelpful question which can invalidate the victims experience and promotes victim shaming. For years, I struggled to understand why I fought so hard to stay with a man who was abusive. As mentioned previously, most people don't recognize non-physical acts of violence as abuse and so it goes unidentified and unspoken about. People don't know what to call their experience, they know it hurts. The silent treatment, for example, is a common abuse tactic used to hurt and control the victim. There is also a certain vulnerability which leaves some susceptible to abuse.

The intermittent periods of good times and special treatment weaved through incidents of abuse adds to the confusing nature of these relationships creating what's known as a trauma bond. A trauma bond is an unhealthy attachment to another person who is also responsible for hurting them. Trauma bonds often cause people to seek healing comfort from the same person who wounded them creating an abuser-rescuer relationship dynamic. As the highs and lows of this break-up- make up cycle continues, each new high creates a new level of hope which serves to strengthen the unhealthy attachment and keeps the cycle going.

There is also a biochemical hooking process that takes place in the brain of a person in a trauma bond. In many cases, the person was love bombed the beginning of the relationship resulting in a rush of happy chemicals called endorphins. Feeling loved, wanted and valued makes us feel good inside. Like an addict, it's easy to get hooked on those good feelings. This is why falling in "love" feels so good. Like an addict, it's easy to get hooked on the good. Unfortunately, when abuse starts the happy chemicals fade. The feeling of love withdrawal may look like anxiety for some and depression for others as we await the return of the love we once knew. Over time, we become appreciative of the most minimal signs of love to soothe us. (See breadcrumbing in chapter 10) As boundaries crumble, the bare minimum soon becomes enough to maintain the relationship.

Chapter 13
Valley Lessons: Narcissistic Abuse and Red Flags of Narcissism

As I stated in my last book, I believe that circumstances will often continue to repeat themselves until the lesson it carries is learned. It's a painful but sometimes necessary medicine. However, there were still factors that I was unaware of that, had I known, may have helped me heal a lot faster and eliminate unnecessary suffering. These are the things I count as lessons.

As a mental health therapist, I assumed that I would have easily recognized toxic relationship patterns common in narcissistic abuse. However, none of my licenses, degrees or titles eliminated my humanness. There are so many people who will not speak up about their experiences out of fear that no one will believe them. My ultimate goal is to spread awareness and to let people know that this kind of abuse is real and actively exists. I used to be concerned about offending people with my story. But my stance now is, if the shoe fits, lace it up tight. It's a sad reality that no one wants to talk about this topic until it hits their house.

As I reflect on my relationship with Love and the lessons I learned, I realize that his decision to walk away from our marriage was a blessing in disguise. It was actually a gift. Of all the gifts he ever gave me, I can truly say that the gift of goodbye was the best one. Had Love never left, I may have never let him go. My loyalty may have kept me in a situation that common sense should have gotten me out of. Sometimes when we refuse to release what's biting us God steps in to shut it down. It hurts but it heals and for that I am thankful.

Being in a pathological love relationship and the divorce taught me many lessons in the valley. Here are a few of my hard lessons learned during this season. If I have helped just one person with my story and knowledge, then my assignment here is complete. Finally, the end of this book includes resources that you can use to educate yourself. You are not crazy and you are not alone.

1. Proving someone to be a narcissist is not as important as recognizing that they are toxic. You don't have to be a narcissist to be toxic. All toxic people are not narcissistic; consequently, all narcissists are definitely toxic

2. If you are like me, you may have doubted that what you experienced was actually abuse. You may have even been ashamed to reveal to others that it was happening.

3. A person's true character is revealed not in how they start a relationship, but how they choose to end one

4. True love shouldn't be exhausting. True love heals. True love protects

5. Stay away from people who consider you expressing how you feel as arguing and being extra. That's a clear indication of gas lighting. Emotionally intelligent people recognize that disagreements don't have to end with arguments or fights

6. No conflict ever gets resolved when dealing with a narcissist. They don't argue with the intent to come to a resolution. They will avoid, deflect, and use word salad leaving you exhausted

7. If someone only loves you when you do exactly what they want and withholds and detaches when you don't behave correctly, that's not love, that's control

8. It's not your fault. Sometimes brave women fall in love with cowards

9. Narcissists are very insecure at their core. They have no sense of inner self. This is why they are able to shift blame without a conscience.

The Story of Tiffany and the Unicorn

I often refer to my life during the valley of divorce as a Tyler Perry movie. Movies that come to mind are "Diary of a Mad Black Woman" and "Why Did I Get Married." Well, what's a good Tyler Perry movie without a good love story and a happy ending? While my story may not have ended exactly like the main characters from Tyler Perry's movies, Helen and Sheila, there were definitely some similarities, particularly as it relates to how they found love in the midst of abandonment and despair. This may not necessarily be the end of my story, but my encounter with Peter was the beginning of a new chapter and a new life full of possibilities. They say that unicorns are fictional creatures that do not really exist...I beg to differ.

It is clear from my moments in the valley that I have made some horrific relationship mistakes. That's why when I met Peter in the middle of my divorce process, I did not give him a second thought. Not only was I still legally married, (I had spiritually divorced myself from Love but that's another book) but I was also in no position to start a romantic relationship with anyone. I was still emotionally broken and needed to heal. So, when I was invited to join a friend, her man, and his friend for a night out, I paused and proceeded with caution. As my depression started to lift, I wrestled in my mind whether it would be a good idea to get out of the house and rejoin society. I passively accepted the invite even though my intentions for showing up were still in question. When I finally arrived at the local restaurant where I was invited, I was 2 hours late.

Peter was a tall, handsome, light-skinned, fine specimen of man with an attractive bone structure and good teeth. He had a beautiful smile and a sexy salt and pepper beard. A tall glass of fifty-something year old wine, I immediately noticed his strong frame as he stood to greet me and gave me his seat. I took one look at Peter and thought to myself, *"Oh lord. Here comes Satan. He wasted no time."* I just knew the devil was coming to finish me off by introducing me to what he knows I physically like in a man. I didn't have to put lipstick on a pig on this one. I was still healing from the trauma associated with my marriage, but I wasn't dead. I kept this in mind throughout the night as I avoided looking at Peter.

We had some drinks and listened to some music. After some small talk and a bite to eat, Peter walked me to my car. After entering my car, I said good night and drove away. No hug, no *when can I see you again,* no exchange of phone numbers. Nothing…and that was exactly the way I wanted it. There were no sparks at the end of the night. I don't know if it was because I had deliberately turned my spark meter off or if sparks were just not there. I struggled to even remember his name the next day.

The next day, I was invited to a cookout where, once again, the four of us would meet up. This cookout would signify the end of a long holiday weekend. We had been out late the night before so I had decided to stay in my makeshift bed for the majority of the day with no intentions of going anywhere. I especially didn't want to go to a cookout where this sexy Rick Foxx look-alike was going to be. So, I declined the invitation. *The devil wasn't about to trap me up,* I told myself after declining the invite. But then I got hungry and all that changed.

I was eventually put in touch with Peter who texted me the address to his cousin's house where the cookout was being held. I rebuked Satan all the way over there as I prepared my mouth to eat good.

We all had a great time. At the end of the night, when everyone left, Peter and I stood outside in his cousin's driveway talking. I learned that, like me, he was from California. He was in Mississippi visiting family between his 4 months on, 2 months off work rotation at a refinery.

"So, what is there to do on a Monday night in Jackson, MS?" He inquired in a familiar California accent.

Peter trailed me to a local spot downtown called Martin's.

"This is not a date," I warned him as we entered.

He laughed, but I was still rebuking the devil. We sat and talked. I told him all about my divorce process and he shared that he too had been divorced. The night ended like the previous one, except this time we exchanged numbers for me to supposedly text him when I made it home. Like the night before, Peter walked me to my car. I entered my car, said good night and drove away. No hug, no 'when can I see you again,' and no sparks, just how I liked it.

The next several weeks were nothing more than occasional telephone calls and texts. Over time this phone communication increased. I was learning a lot about Peter and him a lot about me. He was nice and easy to talk to; however, the guard was still up. Kindness had been what got me caught up with Love in the first place. A few weeks later, my newly found quartet group decided to have a BBQ on the reservoir. Playing it safe, I decided to take my own car and allowed Peter to ride with me. When I stopped at the gas station, Peter stepped out to open my car door for me. By the time he got around to my side I was already out. I wasn't used to that type of treatment. It felt weird. It was even more weird for him to pump my gas and pay for it. When we got back in the car, I immediately went into my purse to give him cash which he did not accept.

"I can put gas in your car," he said laughingly

This too, I was not used to. I had been conditioned to have to pay Love back or be reminded of his contribution to my gas tank at every fight. The other alternative was to settle for a half of a tank and be overly appreciative to save his fragile ego. I didn't need Peter to put gas in my car. But it was still nice. I was still watching for Satan.

Several more weeks passed and it was coming time for Peter to return to work in California. I was enjoying spending time getting to know him, yet I was deliberate about not putting myself in a position where we were alone in private. Up until that point, we had managed not to go beyond a friendly hug. A few days before he was scheduled to leave for California, he invited me to the movies. I agreed but drove my own car.

"This is not a date," I warned again with seriousness in my tone.

"Ok" he said through a chuckle that challenged my serious tone. "This is not a date."

I told myself that this would be me going to the movies with a friend. Maybe thinking of it this way made me feel better and relieved the worry that I was doing something wrong. Even though it had been several months since Love had left me and moved out, I still felt a weird sense of obligation to the marriage during that time as the divorce trial was weeks aways.

I told Peter that I liked scary movies, so that's what we went to see that afternoon. We enjoyed the movie and shared a laugh about the holy oil I brought with me. I wasn't taking any chances with Rick Foxx and I definitely didn't want to take any demons home with me. I offered Peter a drop of my oil as he walked me to my car after the movie. He chuckled as he extended his palm to accept a drop. I got into my car, wished him a good day, and I watched as he walked to his car. I breathed a sigh of relief that we had made it through the day with no sparks; on the contrary, this was about to change. I noticed Peter get back out of his car and watched again as he retraced his steps back to mine.

"I forgot something," he said as he arrived at my partially rolled up window. I rolled my window down further so I could hear him. Peter then leaned into my window and kissed me gently on the cheek. He wished me a good afternoon and walked back to his car. There it was. There was indeed a spark in that moment, but the night ended there.

Peter eventually left and went back to California. We stayed in contact and spoke several times a week. I would hang out with him when he would fly into the city from California but mostly in a group setting. I had to be deliberate about not putting myself in certain situations with him as my fondness of him increased. He became a huge source of support during the ugliest parts of my divorce. There were moments during my process when

I was down on the floor in prayer and devastation. During some of those times, Peter was down on the floor right beside me flipping through the bible trying to find something to sooth me. He never once took advantage of my vulnerabilities during that time, although he had every opportunity to do so. He treated me like a lady; most importantly, he treated me like a friend.

While eventually, our friendship grew and romantic feelings surfaced, I was still fearful. I was on the lookout for red flags that I missed or ignored in Love. I often asked God to remove him from my life if he was sent by the enemy. Peter was not only everything I desired in a man physically, he also demonstrated that he was a protector, a provider and emotionally available which was what I had always desired. He showed that he could communicate through differences. He wasn't afraid to be vulnerable and had tough conversations. Still, I wrestled with whether he was another demonic assignment sent to finish the job Love started. I wondered why he would come into my life *now*?

I did something with Peter that I had failed to do with Love. I got to know him and established a true friendship with him. I am not referring to friends with benefits either; I am referring to a genuine friendship with a person who has no expectations–sexual or financial agendas. Sometimes we are in such a hurry to have our happily ever after that we skip the development of friendship and fast forward right to the wedding. That was certainly the case for me and it cost me a trip back to the valley.

Love would later try to use my developing friendship with Peter as grounds for divorce by accusing me of adultery after he had left the marriage. Although this was not the case, at that point I had lost any interest in what he thought or in proving otherwise. Love's diabolical motives were clear. It was all a game to him and he just wanted to win. He would spend his nights and weekends trying to record phone conversations, capture photos and obtain third party screenshots of my social media page for evidence to use in court. Despite his tricks, I was not spending my time hiding from Love. His accusations were futile and laughable at best. I made a decision that I was going to live and love my life again.

Since the completion of this book, my relationship with Peter has indeed blossomed into romance, a romance that I never saw coming; a romance which began with a genuine friendship. When you have a genuine friendship as your foundation, you will always have that friendship to fall back on during rough patches. When a man can give a woman intimacy without having to remove her clothes, he gives her a great gift. Society has shaped us into believing that in order to heal, we must do so alone. This may be true in certain cases, especially if you are using relationships to avoid the healing process. However, there is a healing power that lies in healthy relationships and connections with others, particularly when you are doing the independent work required to heal. Therapy is a great place to start.

The traumatic effects of my marriage to Love sometimes show up in my relationship with Peter. I am still trying to get adjusted to flowing in my feminine energy and allowing him to protect and provide for me without defaulting to my survival position of needing to be strong all the time. I am adjusting to allowing him to help me without feeling guilty or obligated to reimburse him. I'm learning to trust that we can have a disagreement without it being fatal to our relationship. It feels nice to be able to communicate effectively for the purposes of actually resolving problems. It feels good to be in a space where communicating my feelings is allowed and honored. It feels good to be able to put away my super woman cape some days and not feel like I have to do it all. It feels nice to be protected and cared for. It feels good to be safe.

Most importantly, Peter and Madison have a genuine connection where she is protected and her feelings matter as well. My child is happier than I have ever seen her in the five years I was married to Love which goes to show; who you marry is just as important to your children as it is to you. I don't know what the future holds for me and Peter, but one thing I know for sure is that I will never enter another marriage without consulting God. I don't want to ever have to return to this valley again. I pray that the story of my valley experience helps you to avoid or at best, better navigate the relationship pitfalls that I encountered. I can finally say that I now know love's true identity.

"The truth is that love is supportive and nurturing, not aggressive or demanding. It is protective, not overwhelming. Love expands, gives, and heals."
--Iyanla Vanzant

Literary Resources

Anderson, S. (2014). *The journey from abandonment to healing.* Berkley Books.

Brown, S. L., & Young, J. R. (2018). *Women who love psychopaths: inside the relationships of inevitable harm with narcissists, sociopaths, & psychopaths.* Mask Publishing.

Hoffman, N. (2018). *Is It Me? Making Sense of Your Confusing Marriage: A Christian Woman's Guide to Hidden Emotional and Spiritual Abuse.* Flying Free Media.

Hawkins, D. (2017). *When loving him is hurting you :b hope and help for women dealing with narcissism and emotional abuse.* Harvest House Publishers.

MacKenzie, J. (2015). *Psychopath free: Recovering from emotionally abusive relationships with narcissists, sociopaths, and other toxic people.* Berkley Books.

MacKenzie, J., & Thomas, S. (2019). *Whole Again: Healing Your Heart and Rediscovering Your True Self After Toxic Relationships and Emotional Abuse.* TarcherPerigee.

Pema Chödrön. (2017). *When things fall apart : heart advice for difficult times.* London Thorsons Classics.

Thomas, S., & Choi, C. (2016). *Healing from hidden abuse : a journey through the stages of recovery from psychological abuse.* Mast Publishing House.